PERIL AND A PEPPERMINT PIG

A TINSEL PINE COZY MYSTERY - 1

WENDY MEADOWS

Majestic Owl Publishing LLC
P.O. Box 997
Newport, NH 03773

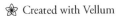 Created with Vellum

CHAPTER ONE

"**A** formal probationary period?" I ask, gaping at the form he slid in front of me seconds before. "You can't be serious, Brogan."

Police Chief Brogan Peterson sits across from me at one of the cozy corner booths at Tinsel Pine's only coffee shop, the Golden Caff. I sit up straighter against the tufted green back of the booth as my one-time boss/possible boyfriend stares me down with steely, uncompromising certainty.

"I'm dead serious, Carol. I'd like to have it signed and notarized by next week, if you're amenable."

And *I'm* about five seconds away from wadding it up and using it to make an improbable shot into the wastepaper basket perched at the edge of the counter. I don't, but more out of respect for the barista working the early evening shift than anything else. It's New Year's Eve, and the shop is ill-equipped to handle the crowds as it is. No need to give the staff extra work on top of dealing with rush hour. But this piece of paper is absolutely trash-worthy, and I'm prepared to tell him so.

"Brogan, I am not going to sign a formal relationship

agreement. This isn't some wacky sitcom. Normal, well-adjusted people don't do this."

"Maybe they should," he argues stubbornly.

I bite back a frosty retort. Brogan isn't like any other man I've dated, for many reasons. The foremost of those being that he's a soon-to-be divorcee still wrapped up in the sticky web of legal proceedings and hurt feelings. His wife has dragged the experience out for six months, trying to gain custody of their Golden Retriever, Columbo. As if she hadn't already taken enough from him.

My own divorce had been fairly simple by comparison. Danny and I grew apart in the absence of our daughter, Mary, who'd been taken from us by her paternal grandparents in a vicious custody battle years before. Danny had chosen to return home to his parents to raise Mary, and I could never fault him for it. I've only just begun to reconnect with my now-adult daughter after moving to the town of Tinsel Pine, Connecticut. My divorce with Danny had been sad, but by the time the split inevitably occurred, we were both ready to let go. I still send him cards on occasion.

But Brogan's wife scandalized everyone by having a torrid extramarital affair right beneath his nose, eventually running off with the town's resident handyman, Seth Gibson. So, I understand where this...*insanity* of Brogan's wells from. But that doesn't mean I have to put up with it.

"Brogan, can't we just enjoy a coffee before I have to go to work?" I wheedle, reaching across the table to take his hand. It's big, blunt-fingered, and calloused from hard labor and an active lifestyle. I give it a gentle squeeze, offering him my sweetest smile.

My smile thaws some of his anger, but the stubborn set of his jaw doesn't ease. "Say you'll sign it at some point and I'll let the subject rest."

Drat. My hope was that being sweet would distract him

enough to realize I'd not given him a direct answer. But I should have known that the chief was too clever for that sort of ploy. How would I get out of this tight spot? If I said no, we'd have a fight. But if I said yes, it meant at some point, I'd need to sign the darn thing. I pride myself on being a woman of my word.

"This is just silly," I mutter. "I just turned fifty, and you're not far behind me. People our age don't do this."

He raises one brow at me. "So that's a no, I take it?"

I lift my cup and drain the dregs of the caramel macchiato so he won't see the gears spinning furiously in my head. I don't have the energy for this fight tonight. I haven't slept well in weeks, and I keep having recurring nightmares about the man who was killed in my house over a month ago now. Poor Gourdy. He hadn't deserved what happened to him.

"I'll think about it," I say finally, setting my cup down on the table, rubbing at the ring it's left on the table rather than meet his eyes. "I'll go ahead and pay now. I need to check in on Mary before I pick up Ms. Adams for the party tonight."

I stand up, slinging the strap of my tote bag over one shoulder, trying my best to ignore the look of disappointment that plays out over Brogan's features. I allow him a few seconds to marshal his expression, letting him think I haven't seen how much my refusal is hurting him. When I glance down hopefully at him thirty seconds later, he's picking irritably at his koozie, expression as bitter as the black coffee in the cup.

I lift the second macchiato I ordered and cram it into the crook of my elbow, covering it with my coat to keep too much steam from leaking out. I don't want to deliver a cup of lukewarm coffee to my daughter. Not after the day she's had.

"Will I see you at the party?" I ask meekly.

His gaze flicks up to my face for just a second before he turns it to glower out the window. "I'll think about it."

And that's my cue to leave. I take it as gracefully as I can, resisting the urge to crane my neck. The curt dismissal will only hurt more if I find he's not watching me go.

The snow is swirling to earth in dizzy spirals, coating the city in a blanket of white. The snow had already been thick on the ground at Christmastime and has worked itself into a proper deluge in the days since. The roads around town have piles of ice and dirty slush built up three or four feet high so the residents of Tinsel Pine can get around in semi-safety. But there is still the ice to contend with, even when the snow is pushed out of the way.

Which is why I am considering calling Ms. Adams to see if she might be able to find an alternate means of transportation to the evening festivities. My two prized horses, Holly and Mistletoe, probably shouldn't be out in this mess. It's just my sort of luck that one of them will fall and be seriously injured. I've just started my sleigh ride business in December and I don't want to hang up my shingle just yet.

I'll just have to see what the weather looks like closer to when I'd planned to pick her up. If nothing else, I can pick her up in my worn but reliable cargo van and refund her the amount for the sleigh ride, excluding gas money.

But right now, I have a daughter to find and console.

Tinsel Pine is a small town, and after a month of running routes through its narrow, homey streets, I know the place by heart. The small strip mall I'll find Mary loitering in is located six blocks from the Golden Caff and a stone's throw away from Tinsel Pine High School.

I spend more time than I care to admit finding a place to secure Holly and Mistletoe, the roan red and magnificent white former racehorses I bought during my first day in Tinsel Pine over a month ago. I finally settle on a bike rack that is dutifully parked outside the flea market and exit the sleigh, smoothing out the folds in my red velvet dress, grimacing at the pronounced curve of my muffin top. Between glazed ham, pecan pies, and a healthy measure of eggnog, I've recently put on more pounds than I like.

The Mrs. Claus costume might be a bit on the nose, I'll admit, but it fits perfectly with the aesthetic of the town. Tinsel Pine, Connecticut celebrates most holidays with equal fervor, with shifting décor and celebrations to adhere to whatever's going on during any given month. But the primary decorations are always Christmas, and with snow still thick on the ground, I'm not doffing the costume yet.

James Nelson, the owner of the flea market and a heavy-set man of below-average height and above-average facial hair, throws me a wink and a wolf-whistle as I pass. Heat flushes into my face, and I tuck a lock of my graying hair behind one ear sheepishly, trying to hide a pleased smile.

I'm not used to the level of male attention I've been getting since arriving in Tinsel Pine. William Gourd, the man whose house I now own, had been the first to press his suit. After he'd passed, I became close to Brogan Peterson, the gruff but charming chief of police. Now James. Where had all these men been during the last twenty years of my life?

Maybe they'd been there, and I was just too busy jet-setting to notice. I spent the better part of those decades behind the wheel of a cargo van, quenching my wanderlust.

I give James a half-hearted wave and a sheepish smile before ducking under the awning of Skye High Jewelry. The awning's teal cloth keeps the worst of the flurries off me as I shoulder the door open.

Skye High Jewelry is a small square that's hardly bigger than the average walk-in closet. Despite this, it makes use of every square inch of the diminutive space, lining the walls with glass cases filled with shining gemstones. They're arranged prettily in settings, but what half of them are called, I can't tell you. Well-educated I might be, but a sophisticate I am not.

Mary has her face pressed against one of the floor-to-ceiling display cases, morosely eyeing a white-gold charm bracelet. I restrain a smile, knowing she won't appreciate the humor I find in the situation. My poor baby has had a day and a half. A little credit card therapy has always been her preferred method of tackling her troubles, a habit she learned from her wealthy and conservative grandmother, Irene.

"I thought I might find you here," I say, sidling up beside her.

Mary jumps a little when my reflection appears in the glass beside hers. Side by side, I can see myself in her, but only just. Mary looks like Danny, built long and gawky, never seeming to gain an ounce no matter how much she eats. Her hair is the same blond I sported until age thirty, when it edged closer and closer to brown. She and I share the same upturned nose and weak chin. Her strong European bone structure is all Danny, though.

"Geez, Mom, don't do that," she says, clutching her chest.

"Do what?"

"Sneak up on me. You're like a cat sometimes. Wear a bell or something."

I ignore the bite of anger in her voice. I know it's not aimed at me, and I've made it a New Year's resolution to get a handle on my temper. Though I suppose I can get away

6

with it for a few hours more. We're not due to watch the ball drop on the community center television until later tonight.

But I offer her a kindly smile and offer her the caramel macchiato I ordered for her. Her irritation seeps away as she snatches it from me and downs half of it in one long pull.

"I thought you could use a pick-me-up," I tell her with a small smile. "I thought I'd try to bolster your nerves before you made an impulse buy."

"Probably wise," she acknowledges with a nod.

"What exactly happened?" I ask, propping my elbow on one cream-colored wall. "I only caught every third word of the voicemail you left. You said something about a mastiff?"

"Rose Fletcher's mastiff, Bruno," Mary growls. "She brought that monster dog into the pet shop today, and she wanted him groomed. He's supposed to be entering some sort of competition soon. Does she warn me he's a runner? No. He just bowls me over the instant she's gone, seizing one of the hamster cages and taking off down Main Street with it!"

I flinch. This is already shaping up to be quite a tale, and I know she's not finished.

"What happened then?"

"What *didn't* happen then?" she says, thunking her head against the glass, leaving a smudge. "Bruno decided to cut off a truck with a horse trailer. It almost jackknifed into the Tinsel Pine Hobby Store and swiped Tom Craft's mid-life-crisis mobile off the road. He was cursing me all the way down the street. Somehow Bruno managed to survive that, though he got slathered in horse hockey. Then he burst into the meeting between Skye Adams and her investors in town hall and shook it off all over her Mont Blancs. She was passing out those Peppermint Pigs that she's been selling for extra cash. Bruno snatched one and kept right on trucking. Skye is furious with me. That's why she's not here."

7

She gestures helplessly to the empty register. Sure enough, Skye's perky blond self is conspicuously absent from the shop. The only other warm body occupying the shop belongs to Vaughn King, the co-owner of the business. He's got his dark head bent over an open ledger, frowning at the numbers printed inside. I let my eyes linger for a minute longer than I should.

Vaughn is a man in his mid-to-late thirties with a head of thinning black hair and an open, welcoming face that escapes being plain by a margin of inches. He pushes his spectacles up his long, thin nose with a frown, muttering darkly to himself.

I can't help but sidle a little closer to him as Mary continues to eye the charm bracelet. Maybe I should buy it for her as an additional and somewhat-belated birthday present. She does have the misfortune of being born on Christmas Day, and thus has the two days shoved together by well-meaning friends more often than not. Business has gone well, and I can afford the excess for once.

"Something wrong?" I ask innocently. I don't want to pry, but he looks upset. I'd gone to Berkeley, pursuing a degree in behavioral therapy. Well-meaning snooping is a bad habit of mine.

Vaughn glances up at me, thin lips quirking in a weary smile. "It's nothing, Miss Green. Just a few inconsistencies in our ledgers. I'm sure I'll get it sorted before the party tonight. Skye said you'd be picking her up. I'm a little relieved, if I'm honest. I'm her back-up ride, and I'm not in the mood for another furious rant."

I let out an inaudible sigh. Well, there goes my plan to bail on Ms. Adams. I can't subject this poor man to an unpleasant evening. He already looks haggard. I'll just make the sleigh ride a leisurely one. Who knows? Skye might appreciate the scenic route.

"I'll be there, eleven o'clock sharp," I promise him, hoisting a bright smile onto my face.

And in the meantime, I have to figure out how to talk my stubborn bull of a boyfriend off the metaphorical ledge before he leaps into outright insanity. *Well*, I console myself. *At least I'm manure-free.*

Sometimes, you have to find the silver lining where you can.

CHAPTER TWO

"It's not as if I'm asking him to move in," I mutter to myself, breath puffing into little clouds in front of my face as I continue the one-sided conversation I've been having with myself for the last fifteen minutes.

It won't be necessary for a while, and we practically live on top of each other anyway. Brogan's house is situated next to the stately yellow home I've bought off Marcy Gourd. We see each other every morning. He brings me my mail most days, for Pete's sake.

I understand his reluctance to commit without boundaries. He's bound to be gun-shy after everything that's happened to him. But the fact that he can't trust me hurts more than I care to admit. We haven't known each other terribly long, so perhaps I'm getting prematurely attached. *Know thyself.* I can admit my faults—even to myself, on occasion. I've grown fond of the churlish policeman in the weeks since we met.

We're a study in contrasts, really. I've lived a life without boundaries, every decision flying in the face of the establishment. A protester at Berkeley, a single divorcee for decades, jet-setting across the U.S. and across the pond for just as long. I'm the antithesis of everything Brogan values. Rules. Order. Rigid standards of right and wrong.

Maybe *I'm* the problem. Because when I think of signing the document, it makes me feel *claustrophobic*; trapped in a cramped space with my insecurities and no escape. Maybe the stifling constraint of a relationship would split us apart, leaving us with nothing but crackling animosity. I don't think I can take that.

My eyes drop to my wristwatch again as I rub my hands together. Even with the thick woolen gloves on, my hands are starting to stiffen in the cold. I'm looking forward to the cozy confines of the community center and the glass of mulled cider that awaits me there.

Skye Adams is almost fifteen minutes late. When she fails to emerge straight away, it doesn't alarm me unduly. Punctuality has never been my strong suit, either, so I can't throw stones at Ms. Adams for it. But when five minutes morph into ten, and then fifteen, I begin to worry. Is she planning to emerge at all? At this rate, she's going to miss the party that she has a hand in orchestrating.

I dig my phone out of my tote bag and check to make sure I've not missed a call. When I unlock the screen, I don't see any missed messages. Strange. Maybe my texts haven't gone through and she doesn't realize I'm here. Signal can be spotty when the weather is miserable, the way it is tonight. The midnight sky spits fat flurries into my face, numbing my cheeks and clinging tenaciously to my eyelashes. I blink them away furiously.

I can just picture her pacing the floor, tiny feet slapping along her hardwood. She'll shake her head, tossing those tight blond curls in disgust, full lower lip curling.

After another five minutes pass, I decide to check on her. I'm expecting to find a haughty note on her door that explains she's taken Vaughn's offer for a ride when I failed to provide prompt customer service.

Skye Adams owns a cottage-style home that's situated on a cramped square of green grass. It's barely got enough room to accommodate a swing set. It surprises me, in all honesty. Skye seems to take pride in maintaining the illusion of an affluent business owner. From her hundred-and-fifty-dollar footwear to the diamond and white-gold earrings, she's every inch a classy lady.

So why the modest home? It seems utterly incongruous.

Pushing aside my nosy impulses, I mount the two cement steps that lead up to her door and knock.

"Ms. Adams?" I call. "Ms. Adams? Can you hear me? It's me, Carol Green. You booked a sleigh ride this evening. I'm here to pick you up."

There's only frosty silence from the other side of the door. She's probably glaring daggers at me from the other side, deciding whether to demand a refund. I err on the side of politeness, though the delay isn't solely my fault.

"I'm sorry to keep you waiting, Ms. Adams. The weather held me up for a little while."

Still nothing. Frowning, I try the doorknob. Maybe she can't hear me.

I push the door open just an inch or two. I may dislike boundaries, but I'm not a complete boor. "Ms. Adams?"

My own voice echoes back to me from the interior of the house. I peek my nose around the side of the door and discover, to my surprise, that the living room beyond is mostly pitch-black, only lit by the blank blue of a television without signal. I don't see her anywhere. Surely if she's home, she would have more lights on?

I push the door open a foot, easing my curvy frame through the door to stand on the welcome mat. There's a slice of light that slashes through the gloom from the door to the kitchen. I hesitate before padding toward it. I've about decided she's not home, and the least I can do is leave her refund on the counter or plastered by a magnet to her fridge.

I pad over the plush carpet, skirting around a coffee table. I nearly turn a plastic dump truck into a skate when I accidentally step on it. I catch myself on the wall with a small yelp, pausing to let my heart resume a normal rhythm before pulling the kitchen door open.

The kitchen is small, barely escaping the definition of a kitchenette. A little card table is pushed into one corner by the window. The dishwasher and stove are pressed together like uneasy allies, hemmed in by a short length of countertop and cabinets.

There's barely enough room in the place for a family to sit. Which is why I can't miss the figure sprawled out on the floor in front of me. Skye Adams lies sprawled on the linoleum floor, hair obscuring most of her lovely heart-shaped face.

My heart throws itself at my ribs in fright. I drop to my knees beside her, pushing her hair back so I can get at her neck. I pray to God it's an accident, that she'll be okay.

But it's a futile effort. She's cool to the touch, almost as frigid as the air outside. No pulse of life thrums against my probing fingers.

Skye is dead, and has been for a while.

I squeeze my eyes shut. *No, no, no. This can't be happening again. Wasn't it bad enough I'd discovered a body my first day here in Tinsel Pine?* Surely one corpse per year was more than enough.

It takes me a few minutes to collect myself enough to reach into the tote bag and fish out my phone. I dial the number with shaking fingers and cross my fingers tightly, praying Brogan will pick up.

The phone rings heartlessly several times. When Brogan

finally picks up, he greets me with a gruff bark of, "What? I'm not in the mood for another argument, Carol. So if you're trying to convince me to drop it, you can just—"

"Skye Adams is dead."

Brogan stops mid-tirade, stunned into silence by my abrupt pronouncement.

"What?"

"Skye Adams is dead," I repeat, voice quavering. "I just found her, Brogan. She booked an appointment with me, and I kept waiting for her to show. After twenty minutes went by and I hadn't seen her, I went inside her house to check. I found her in her kitchen. She's cold, Brogan. I think she's been gone for a while."

"Can you spot signs of a struggle?" Brogan asks, shifting immediately into the cold, analytical mindset of a detective, his earlier irritation set aside for now.

I scan the kitchen again, trying to drink in any details I missed. Most of my attention fixes immediately on Skye's prone form. Aside from a few wrinkles in her normally pristine blazer, she appears unruffled. It's as if she just keeled over dead unexpectedly.

My eyes land on the pile of broken pink shards that lie a few feet from Skye's questing fingers. Most of it appears decimated, ground into tiny flecks. But enough of the porcine head remains that I can make out what it must have been. Skye died clutching one of her precious peppermint pigs.

"I don't see anything," I admit, filing the odd sight away for later consideration. "It's like she just...died, Brogan."

"Could be an accident," Brogan says with a sigh. "Or a health issue. Heart attack, aneurysm, and so on. I'm still going to need to come out there with a squad of first responders. You okay to stay put?"

I nod, realizing a moment later that he can't see me and

mumble an affirmative. All the anticipation for tonight's party has drained away like yesterday's bathwater, leaving me cold. I don't think I can pry myself away from this chilling sight even if I try.

Brogan promises to arrive in a few minutes and hangs up. I don't even bother to be angry about his compulsive need not to say goodbye. I just stare numbly at Skye. So still, so peaceful in death.

Maybe he's right; maybe it's an accident. Only time and testing can tell. But I don't think so. A nagging feeling in my gut tells me it's something more sinister. I think she was murdered.

And the only witness is the shattered peppermint pig on the floor.

CHAPTER THREE

"Are you drunk?" I ask, staring disbelievingly at Brogan's stern profile.

Between the wintery mix and the compacted ice already on the ground, it took Brogan and his men almost an hour to turn up. An hour I spent on the stoop of Skye's tiny home. It was just too macabre to hunch over her body like a voyeur.

Brogan scowls down at the coffee cup in his hand, shoved hastily into his grasp by Officer Dawson a few minutes ago. I assumed, at first, it was to bolster him. Now I realize it's to sober him up.

"Tipsy," he grumbles, bringing the cup to his lips. "Excuse me for indulging a little holiday cheer on New Year's Eve. This was supposed to be my night off."

It's more than that, and we both know it. This has as much to do with our fight as it does the holiday. We sit in stony silence for a while, until the sound of the small grandfather clock Skye has shoved in a corner chimes the midnight hour. The sound echoes mournfully through the interior of the dark house, robbing me of the last vestiges of my anger. Poor Brogan. He hasn't had an easy day, has he?

I offer him my hand, a peace offering. He contemplates it for a second or two before taking it and giving it a gentle squeeze. With the other, he sets the coffee aside with a sigh.

"Sorry. This is all just...too much, Carol. I shouldn't be snapping at you."

"And I'm sorry that you're here, stuck on a porch in the cold waiting for forensics instead of enjoying the cider," I say. "We missed the ball drop. I know everyone was looking forward to it."

Apparently, it's something of a tradition in Tinsel Pine to attend the community center party, get well and truly schnockered, and watch the start of the New Year play out live on the widescreen television mounted on the wall. For my part, I'd been looking forward to kissing him again.

Brogan shrugs. "You did the right thing in calling me. The longer she lays here, the less evidence we're likely to get. I just wish there was more at the scene. Bill's murder last month was pretty clear-cut—strangulation is pretty hard to miss. But this..." He trails off with another sigh. "It's scary, is what it is. This sort of thing shouldn't happen in towns like Tinsel Pine. Until last month, the closest thing we had to murder on record was a hit-and-run on a backroad near the border to Glovin County, and we actually found the guy."

Though it's completely ludicrous, a pang of guilt twists my gut. These things didn't start happening until I got here. Who's to say it's not a sign? I'm not a hugely superstitious person, but I do believe in karma, in fate, in the guiding will of the universe, what have you. I can't shake the unnerving thought that it's somehow my fault.

Brogan nudges my chin up with two fingers, a bleak smile stretching his lips. The tender touch warms me just a little, but I can't completely brush aside my silly premonition.

"Hey, what's that look for?"

"I'm just sorry, is all. For all of this."

"Unless you're the murderer, you have nothing to be sorry for, Carol. You're doing good by calling us in." He glances around and lowers his voice to a mere whisper. "Chin up, you hear? You helped us last time, and I'd like you to do it again. I need you sharp, to keep a keen ear to the ground. Can you do that for me?"

I blink at him a couple of times in surprise. During the last murder investigation, he kept rejecting help. Now he wants me on this? Why?

"I'm not sure it's strictly appropriate, sir," I hedge. "After all, you sort of have a conflict of interest where I'm concerned. I am your girlfriend, after all. Unless that's changed?"

The weighty statement hangs in the air for a second, but Brogan ultimately bats it away like a cat toy, not rising to the bait.

"Can you do it or not?"

I nod slowly. "I can. What sort of gossip would you like me to collect?"

"All of it. Anything that sounds pertinent or promising. Heck, even the stuff that's not. You never know what details might lead to something. The only thing we currently have in evidence is that pig, and who really knows what that's supposed to mean?"

"I do, actually," I say, stealing the coffee cup from his hands. He stares at me in unflattering shock, as though I've started spouting Pig Latin.

"Don't give me that look, Brogan. I'm more than a pretty face with a keen ear for gossip. I'm also exceptionally well-traveled. You don't spend nearly twenty years on the road and pick up nothing. The peppermint pig tradition originates in Saratoga, New York."

Brogan pushes up from his position on the step as a black SUV pulls up to the curb outside of Skye's home. The driver —a balding, overweight man with watery eyes—considers Holly and Mistletoe, completely nonplussed. I take it as our cue to go and pull Brogan toward the lacquered sleigh as I explain myself.

"It started in the 1880s. Jim Mangay wanted to make something like marzipan candy. But marzipan wasn't available, so he improvised, using peppermint oil from his father's apothecary. They went the way of the dodo for a while because of sugar rationing during the World Wars. Then about a hundred years later, someone found the original mold and started producing them again. It's been a tradition ever since. It's gaining traction all over the world."

Brogan hums thoughtfully as I snap the reins, spurring the horses into motion. I continue, filling him in on the only other things I know for certain at this point.

"They're usually sold with a hammer, and the pig is shared between a group, each person breaking off a piece of pig for good luck in the New Year."

Brogan's unhappy snort sounds eerily like one of Mistletoe's. "Well, it didn't bring Ms. Adams much luck, did it?"

"I suppose not. All I know is that she was selling them to her investors. She was kind of a crafty person. She was selling ornaments to them around Christmastime."

He taps his chin. "That tidbit about the hammer is interesting, though. About how big are they?"

I spaced my fingers about five inches apart. "They're not huge, but they're generally made of glass. They could do the job of killing a person if needed."

Still, that doesn't seem right to me. Nothing else in the

house is broken, so far as I can tell. Just Skye, who'd been busy breaking apart her pig when the mysterious death occurred. No muss, no fuss. Blunt-force trauma doesn't seem right.

I keep the thought to myself, though. If it warms Brogan to think he's gotten a lead, I'm not divesting him of the feeling. I've thoroughly ruined his evening without being a Debbie Downer as well.

"Let's get you home," I say, forcing some cheer into my tone.

We say little on the way back to our respective homes. Brogan, in his usual fashion, does not say goodbye before stalking up to his front door. I examine his front door with its peeling paint and antique doorknob for a long time, even after his lights have flickered off, wondering just what I'm going to do with this taxing man.

My guess at the moment? Get ourselves in trouble solving a murder.

CHAPTER FOUR

B rogan and I don't see or speak to each other for
another week and a half.

I want to blame it on the murder investigation.
Once again, a mysterious death has all of Tinsel Pine in an
uproar, clamoring for justice. Brogan has to appear to be
doing something, even if there's little he can do until the
mortician's findings and the toxicology report show up on
his desk.

And yet, he hasn't returned any of my late-night calls or
texts. Not even the innocuous ones, like "hello" or "I miss
you." Who is too busy to even say hello?

I examine my irritation with the police chief during the
odd moments I'm alone, which isn't often. Even at home,
there's Mary, who seems to have taken Skye's loss very hard. I
hadn't realized they were so close after only a few weeks. I
suppose she spent more time in that outlet mall than I ever
dreamed. She seems set on comforting Vaughn whenever she
can, bringing him over several nights out of the week.

It seems heartless for me to bring up my personal
problems with Brogan when so much is going on. So I go

about my business, ferrying the residents of Tinsel Pine to and from their destinations. I keep my promise to Brogan, filing away as many tidbits as I can for later use if Skye turns out to have been murdered.

There's a particularly juicy conversation going on in the back of the sleigh as I stare out at the road, brooding. I give myself a mental shake and force myself to pay attention.

The two women in the back look to be in their mid-thirties, with matching bob-style haircuts and knit hats that are all fashion and don't help with the cold one bit. The first is slightly taller than her companion, her hair blond and hanging straight as a ruler. The other is a brunette with more spring in her shiny locks than her height-advantaged companion.

I swear I've seen them before, though I struggle to place where. They listed their names as Nina Marshall and Diane Simmons on the sign-up sheet. They're huddled over a copy of the *Tinsel Pine Herald*, the small but aggressively persistent newspaper in town. I've declined to comment about Skye Adams's death three times in quick succession.

"Hush, Nina," Diane says, slapping her friend lightly on one arm. I doubt she feels much through the layers the puffy pink coat provides. "You can't go saying things like that! People will hear!"

But the joyous sing-song in her tone convinces absolutely no one. Nina continues the conversation I've been tuning out.

"It has to be Tom Craft."

Nina purses her lips, hiding a smile, but goes on playing devil's advocate. "We don't know it's murder yet. The police haven't issued a statement."

Nina rolls her eyes and attempts to pull the knit cap down over her pink ears, trying in vain to warm them. "Well, I'm calling baloney on the heart attack theory. She was only thirty-eight, and if she skipped the gym a day in her life, I'll eat my hat. Someone killed her. And I think it was Tom."

"I hate to be nosy, but who's Tom?" I ask, craning my neck, taking my eyes off the road for a few seconds. This side road isn't well-traveled, so I think we'll all be safe. The snow has cleared up some in recent days, so I've had to take the off roads.

The women jerk as though I've startled them.

Diane recovers from the shock first and smiles sheepishly. "Sorry for distracting you, Ms. Green. We don't mean to be horrible gossips. We'll quiet down."

For the first time since starting my business, I tell an outright falsehood to one of my customers. I force a smile onto my face and give an easy shrug. "I don't mind gossip."

In truth, I mind it a whole lot. Loose, malicious tongues maligned me to my daughter for most of her life. I don't like the rumor mills that run day and night in small, insular communities. But this is what Brogan needs from me. He needs someone to whom people feel comfortable telling secrets.

Nina leans forward with a conspiratorial smile. "Tom Craft is a veterinary assistant at the Four Legacy Animal Clinic in Glovin County. He's also a horrible womanizer and Skye's ex-husband. If anyone has a motive, it's him. I hear the custody case has been dragging on for almost a year now."

She's right. It *does* sound like an excellent motivator for murder. Somehow, I don't think that it's going to go over well with Brogan, though. The chief will probably feel some measure of sympathy, as a man who is also going through a divorce.

"Looks like he gets the kids by default now," Diane says with a solemn nod. "Only one parent left. Though if Rose

Fletcher gets her way, she'll install herself as the wicked stepmother soon enough."

"Rose Fletcher?" I echo, trying to piece together where I've heard the name. I know it's familiar somehow.

"Tom's newest flame," Nina says with a nod. "Enough force of personality to choke a bear. She may just get her wish and marry that man. I don't know who I'll feel sorry for the most if that happens—Tom, Rose, or the kids."

"Definitely the kids," Diane mutters.

The pair ask for one more loop around town before I let them off at their stop. Both wave to me as I pass, but I can barely muster up enough concentration to return it. Because I've finally put my finger on why the name sounds familiar.

Rose Fletcher owns the mastiff that escaped Mary not so long ago. At the time, it had just seemed like a zany and unfortunate tale she'll laugh about in months to come. Now I'm not so sure.

Is it just coincidence that the woman stealing Skye's husband owns a dog that stole one of her prized pigs?

And is it also possible that said woman also stole Skye's life?

I knock on Brogan's door after the sun goes down; my last two customers of the night are safely away, and my horses are safe in their stable.

The walk over is frigid, and I'm shaking from head to toe by the time the door swings inward.

"What?" he barks, glaring at me from the gap.

Brogan is still in uniform, though he's missing a gun belt, and three of the buttons around the collar are undone. His hair is flattened to his skull after repeated mussings, and the bags beneath his eyes are a scary leaden color that foretell a state of surliness yet unknown to mankind. Brogan is already like a bear with a sore head on good days, with only flashes of good humor to indicate there's something other than pure spite flowing through his veins. I'm afraid I'll have to stick my hand up one nostril and root around in the depths of his brain to drag that man out now.

I've already turned half away from the door, convinced it's a bad idea to be here, when Brogan catches my wrist and drags me to a halt. My heels grind audibly on the salt he's thrown out onto the porch.

"Don't go," he says quietly. "I'm sorry for snapping."

"It's fine," I mumble. "We can talk when you've had a chance to sleep."

"I'll sleep when I'm dead. Come in. You're as cold as ice."

I glance pointedly at the sunny yellow siding of my stately home looming above his more modest ranch-style house. Covered in a light dusting of snow, it looks like a candied treat or something you'd find in a children's storybook. Not the site of a murder only a month back.

"I can warm up at home. I don't want to bother you if it's a bad time."

Brogan doesn't release his grip on my arm and mutters something unintelligible before reeling me into his chest. Though he's only about a decade younger than I am, he's in much better shape. The contours of the chest splayed beneath my fingers and cheek are more impressive than even the tight cut of the police uniform hints at. He buries his face in my hair.

"Don't go," he repeats. "It's been a bad day, and I could use the company."

I finally soften to him, relenting with grace as he pulls me inside and shuts the door. It's then that I get my first glimpse of his place. In the few weeks we've been dating, we've always met at my home, the police station, or the Golden Caff. It's a subject I've never had the courage to broach with him until now.

The interior is a lot lighter than I expect from a man like Brogan. The walls are done in maple paneling, offset by blue-gray carpet and cornflower curtains. The couches and armchairs are ivory and bunched around a coffee table in the middle of the room. A small mantle hovers over an electric fireplace, and a dozen or so frames perch atop it. Only six of them are visible, containing photographs of what look to be Brogan's dog, Columbo, or his aging parents. The other six are pushed face down and, though I can't see them, I have a feeling I know who they frame.

Brogan pushes me down onto the couch and shuffles toward the kitchen.

"I'm going to get coffee. Would you like anything?"

"Coffee would be excellent, thank you," I say quietly, some of my confidence robbed by this place and the presence of the woman who clearly helped shape it. There's a part of me—and I'm a little ashamed of how potent it is—that wants to flip the photos up and stare at the face of the woman who's caused so much misery.

Brogan reemerges from the kitchen, clutching two ceramic mugs full of coffee. He sets one on the table for me before downing half of his own. He doesn't even seem to care about the scalding temperature. I wrap my fingers around the mug gratefully before settling back into the cushions with a sigh.

"So, what did you come to tell me?"

My eyes flick back to the mantle for a half-second and I wonder if I ought to tell him. We've avoided a fight about his relationship agreement thus far. Would telling him stir up all his earlier ire? But I'm all in now, and I'm keeping him from sleep for no purpose if I don't spill what I know.

"I kept an ear out for gossip, just like you said. The general consensus seems to be that Tom Craft had the most to gain from Skye's death."

Brogan nodded absently. "That tracks with what we've suspected. Murders are often perpetrated by someone the victim knows."

I latch onto the slip he's made at once and ask in a hushed whisper, "So it is a murder?"

His lips thin into an unhappy line as he realizes what he's done. "Sometimes I hate just how astute you are, Carol. It's going to get you into trouble one of these days. Trouble I might not be around to protect you from."

I flap a hand in the air and disguise my satisfied smile by taking another slurp of coffee from my mug. Brogan's added chicory to the mix, along with the cream and sugar, giving it a rather woodsy flavor that I like. "No backsies, Brogan."

He finishes off his coffee in another long draft and sets it down on his coaster with a clink. "It was murder. Someone spiked the wine she was drinking with a lethal dose of Tramadol. The drugs had a severe interaction and suppressed her nervous system."

"In plain English?"

"It inhibited her heart and lungs' ability to breathe and beat. Not enough oxygen to the brain, which resulted in brain death, with the rest of the body following suit not long after."

I shudder. Poor Skye. No matter how difficult she could be at times, she hadn't deserved that death.

"So it was planned," I muse, trying to ignore the vivid mental pictures his words paint. "Not a crime of passion, the way it was with Gourdy last month."

"We're looking for a stone-cold killer," he confirms. "Someone who could get close and who had access to

29

medications like Tramadol. Someone like a doctor or a veterinarian."

"Or a vet tech," I say quietly.

We exchange a glance. Brogan's face is as serious as I've ever seen it, and I know we're thinking the same thing.

"We need to pay a visit to Tom Craft."

CHAPTER FIVE

The Four Legacy Animal Clinic is technically out of Brogan's jurisdiction, so it's up to me to approach Tom Craft in his place of employment. My stomach is a riot of nerves as I pull my beat-up cargo van to a stop in the gravel parking lot.

What I'm doing could get me in a lot of trouble. Potentially lethal trouble, if Tom Craft really is our murderer. If we're right about his guilt, he could attack me. As a man in the prime of his life, he can overpower a shorter, fifty-year-old, slightly overweight woman with ease. I don't want to die the way Skye did, struggling to breathe on the floor.

Brogan is counting on you, I remind myself. *And Skye deserves justice. Just hoist up your girdle and do this, Carol.*

Appropriately chided, I duck my head and exit the van, stepping into the chilly January air with a grimace.

The clinic has been modeled to look like a grouping of rustic cabins closed off by chain-link fences. A closer look at the siding reveals it's all imitation materials and not a speck of actual wood has gone into the construction of the long, squat buildings. The entire set-up is situated on a sixty-acre plot designed to house animals of all shapes and sizes. It's officially the only no-kill shelter around, so it has many, many inhabitants at present.

My black shorthair, Stockings, pokes her head out of my tote bag when she hears a chorus of meows coming from just beyond the door. I stroke her between her fuzzy ears for a bit as I step through the glass door, which has been propped open a few inches by a dusky orange brick.

The odor of dozens of pets, medication, and cleaner hits me in an aromatic wave, and it takes me a few seconds to adjust. By the time I blink my eyes open again, a girl Mary's age or younger is standing in front of me, clipboard in hand, offering me a genial smile. Her shiny plated name tag reads, "Helen."

"Hello there," she enthuses. "You must be our two o'clock, Carol and Stockings."

I force a smile as well, though I'm sure it's not got the wattage that Helen's has. "That's us."

Helen bends to be on Stockings's level and strokes behind her ears in a manner that has my cat purring in an instant. "What a little cutie we've got here. Are you sure you're just here for a wellness check? Has she got her shots?"

"I'm sure." I don't tell her that this cat originally came from Marcy Gourd's pet store in Tinsel Pine and that all her animals are up to date on their vaccinations before being sold.

"Well, have a seat," Helen instructs, waving her hand at the small lobby area set to the side of the door. "Tom will be out before too much longer to escort you back."

Tom Craft? If it's really him, this has exceeded my hopes. My original plan was to stick around and try to get him alone. But if he's our tech, I'll have at least five to ten minutes in which we can speak without interruption.

I settle myself and my tote back onto the bench seating

that lines the lobby. There are six other people waiting at the moment. A set of late teenaged twins with matching corgipoos settled at their feet, an elderly man with a cockatiel perched on his shoulder, a little girl curled into her mother's side with a rabbit in a cage on her lap, and a woman in her mid-thirties who's half-wrestling her giant mastiff.

Wait a second. A mastiff? Exactly how many of those could be running around Tinsel Pine or Glovin County? It's not exactly a compact animal. They can range anywhere from a hundred and fifty to two hundred and forty pounds, meaning most male mastiffs are heavier than me. And of those mastiffs, how many have spritely female owners like this one?

I examine the woman more closely. She has her dark mahogany hair piled up on top of her head in a haphazard fashion. She's pale, harried, and looks almost as tired as Brogan these days. She's a little thing, barely over five feet tall, with a petite frame and the musculature of a cooked spaghetti noodle. How she's managing to keep the dog in place is anyone's guess.

My suspicions are confirmed when I hear her hiss, "Behave, Bruno! This is not the time!"

So this is Rose Fletcher, the woman Diane and Nina were discussing yesterday in the back of my sleigh. She wouldn't normally stand out to me in a crowd as a homewrecker. Only force of personality boosts a rather plain face into anything of note. As I watch, she levels a glare at the pair of twins, as though it's their fault her dog is misbehaving.

I'm contemplating moving closer to speak to her when the door opens and a man sticks his head through the gap. I pause to admire the view because, even though I don't like him, I can see why Skye and Rose might. Tom Craft is a looker. He's got the body of a gymnast. Broad-shouldered, with a chiseled torso, lean-cut waist, and rippling muscle evident even under the pair of tan scrubs he wears. His face is just as impressive as the body. Square jaw, sweeping cheekbones, full mouth, and heavy brows set over smoldering brown eyes, and a mouth that looks intriguingly kissable.

It's not a wonder that all members of the female persuasion in the lobby, aside from the little girl, look up and take note.

His eyes scan the room, lingering for a protracted second on Rose, who's still struggling with her mastiff. She's only half paying attention to Bruno now, too busy staring soppily up at Tom like he's an action star come to save her. Rose Fletcher has fallen hard for Mr. Craft, and it's apparent to anyone who's looking for more than a few seconds. It almost makes me feel bad for the woman because Tom does not look as happy to see her as she does to see him.

"Tom," she mouths and tries to wave him over with one hand, releasing one of the mastiff's bulky shoulders. "Tom, come here."

Tom slides his eyes away from her and slaps a patently false smile onto his face, ignoring the plea with heartless professionalism. "Ms. Green?"

I push up from my seat, keeping a hold of Stockings as I make my way over to him. He's just lifted Stockings into those unfairly muscular arms when all hell breaks loose in the lobby.

Bruno surges forward, claws skittering on the tile of the lobby, trailing his leash behind him. Even with his unsure footing, he manages to cross the space to the little girl's side in one massive bound, taking the handle of the rabbit's cage in his teeth and swinging it up with a happy bark. Then he hurtles toward Tom and knocks into him with the force of a battering ram, taking him out at the knees. Stockings goes flying out of his arms, and I barely have enough time to catch her before she goes sailing over the counter.

My heart beating sledgehammer blows into my ribcage, I clutch the terrified cat to my chest and wrap her in my coat for safekeeping. I feel a little better once feel her body purring softly against mine.

The little girl's wail fills the lobby, and I turn just in time to see the mastiff shoulder open the door and take off into the January afternoon like a shot. Too late…I remember Mary's tale about Bruno's other misadventure. If the dog is allowed to run off, he'll hide or abandon the rabbit someplace unfortunate, and end up traumatizing a little girl for life. Rose is too busy crouching over Tom's body to catch her fleeing pooch, and the rest of the crowd seems frozen in shock. So I suppose it's up to me.

"Hold her," I mutter to Tom, who has managed to push himself up onto his elbows. I plop Stockings gently onto his chest and waddle after the renegade canine as fast as the compacted snow, ice, and my own heavy wardrobe will allow.

I'm reminded of just how out of shape I am with every breath. The cold air slices at my insides like a knife, and a nasty taste enters my mouth as I breathe raggedly in and out. Mary is a dedicated jogger, and were she here, she'd helpfully point out that my current discomfort is a result of my sedentary lifestyle. Intense exercise puts pressure on the lungs, which can push blood into the air sacs of the lungs, causing a filmy, metallic taste. Hence why I should run more.

I shoot a quick bargain to the big man upstairs. If I can somehow catch this dog and save the rabbit, I'll start running every day with Brogan and Mary, my resolution to relax in the New Year be darned.

The Four Legacy Animal Clinic is bordered on one side by old-growth forest, and this is the direction that the mastiff homes in on. I have to stop him before he gets into the trees. If I'm forced to take this chase over gnarled roots, I'm sure to break my neck.

"Bruno!" I shout, trying to catch the dog's attention. He skids to an uneasy stop, sending snow flying in an arc around him. The rabbit's cage swings lightly in his jaws, and he wags his tail energetically as if this is all a big game.

I reach into my coat pocket and withdraw a packet of cat treats Mary sold to me just two days before. They're Stockings's favorite, and I can never seem to keep enough in the household. In lieu of a grandchild, I spoil my cat. Sue me.

Bruno's eyes lock onto the bag of treats, and the tail wagging reaches a new frenetic pace, jiggling his whole backside with good cheer.

"Want these, boy?" I call in a frantic sing-song.

More tail wagging.

"Drop the cage, and you can have some treats."

Bruno understands the word "treats" because, as soon as the word is uttered, he lets the handle of the cage slide through his teeth and comes bounding toward me. I have only a half-second to pivot out of the way of his full weight before he's in front of me, buffeting against the side of my legs, body quivering like a furry subwoofer. Even the partial contact is enough to knock me end-first into the snow.

Bruno descends on me with a large, wet tongue, giving me doggy kisses against my objections. After being positively showered in spittle, I manage to press the dog onto his side, holding him in place with my one-hundred-and-sixty-pound frame as best I can while he gobbles up my cat's treats.

I'm stuck like that for who-knows-how-long until help arrives. Helen, Tom Craft, Rose Fletcher, and the mother with her sobbing daughter crowd around me sometime later. Their voices overlap, a jumble of apologies and "thank yous", but I don't respond to any of it until Rose has gotten her dog bundled up into the backseat of her Ford Escape.

"I'm so, so sorry," she babbles. "I don't know what happened."

She'd let go, that's what happened, but I can't say for sure if it was intentional or not. I wave her off, unable to force myself to smile at her at the moment. I take Tom's offered hand, and he helps me to my feet, brushing snow off my jacket.

Maybe it's the week apart from Brogan, but I can't help but be a little bit enthralled by the spicy scent of Tom's aftershave. I hastily step away from him just as soon as I'm capable.

"We're really sorry, Ms. Green," he says, parroting Rose's words. "I should have grabbed Bruno before he took off. Is there anything we can do to make any of this up to you? Don't worry about your visit today. The doctor says it's on the house after this."

I seize the offered opportunity with both hands.

"It would mean a lot to me if I could take your children for a snow ride, Mr. Craft," I say, adopting the most somber tone I can manage. "Free of charge. I was looking for a delicate way to ask, but I really think it could do them some good. After what happened to poor Ms. Adams..."

I trail off, letting the statement hang. Tom's face goes curiously blank for a few seconds, like a computer screen awaiting input. After a couple of seconds' calculations, his brain must have finally spit out the idea to smile because he does so, slowly and unconvincingly.

"That sounds lovely, Ms. Green. But I couldn't—"

"I simply insist," I say, wiping Bruno's spittle off my face for emphasis as if to say, "Look at what you still owe me, punk."

Tom's gaze flits around the circle, and I see it when he declares surrender. His shoulders slump as he realizes he's being watched. Rudely turning me down would result in still more talk.

"Alright," he says, voice strained. "I guess I'll schedule that with you sometime this week after my in-laws have a chance to clear out."

"Wonderful."

Things wind down after that. The mother and daughter pair with the rabbit disappear, taking their furry problems elsewhere. The teenagers are in furious conversation with the cockatiel-owner. I'm chivvied back with Stockings within minutes of being escorted inside, taken toward the back by Helen this time.

I catch a brief snippet of conversation before the door to the lobby closes. Rose Fletcher and Tom Craft are speaking in low voices, hoping not to be overheard.

"We have to talk, Tom," she hisses.

"Not now, Rose. I'm at work. We agreed. Your mutt ruined everything."

"My *mutt?* How dare you, Thomas James Craft! It was your idea to train him to snatch things, not mine. Don't blame me when things go sour."

"He's useless," Tom hisses. "If he'd done what he was supposed to, no one would have had to get hurt. Instead, she forced me to play hardball."

My heart kicks up another notch. *She? Does he mean Skye? Who else can he mean?*

But I never get to hear the remainder of the conversation because the door swings shut, cutting me off from their conversation and leaving me literally—and metaphorically—in the dark.

CHAPTER SIX

T om Craft ultimately decides to get his obligatory sleigh ride done on Friday after Tinsel Pine Elementary School lets out early due to weather.

Tom has two children, a boy and a girl named Clark and Serena. Clark turns nine soon, or so he mumbles to me when we make our introductions. Serena is only six and doesn't say much at all, gripping her brother's hand as if it's the only thing tethering her to earth. She looks everywhere but at me, even as she climbs into the back of the sleigh. I offer the pair some cookies, but neither seem to have much of an appetite.

The pair have a sort of dull, dead-eyed stare that makes it seem as though they're looking straight through everything and seeing none of it. It makes my chest ache. How much do they understand about what's happened? I can only hope the answer is very little.

Tom looks just as annoyed as he did during my clinic visit. He keeps staring over my head as if he's checking an imaginary clock.

"Did everything work out with Bruno?" I inquire

pleasantly, peeking over my shoulder to watch Tom's reaction as Holly and Mistletoe begin trotting forward.

He jerks a little in his seat, surprised by the question. He recovers himself quickly, though.

"Yeah, Bruno turned out just fine. You did a great job with him the other day, by the way. You ever think of going into veterinary work, Ms. Green? You seem to have a way with animals."

"I've got all the animal company I need right here. Don't I, Stockings?" I croon, scratching Stockings beneath her chin. She's curled up on the passenger's side of the cushioned sleigh bench. She lifts her head, deigning to let me pet down her front, and purrs.

"You have a pretty kitty," Serena says quietly. "Mommy had a kitty like that once, but it died. Just like mommy."

The words slide between my ribs and twist like a knife, making my heart ache. Poor, poor little girl. It's even worse because it's stated in a matter-of-fact tone, without tears or even the trembling lower lip that always kills me.

I turn my head back after taking a turn in time to see Tom glower at Serena. She shrinks away from him, pressing her back in a line against the side of the sleigh, going white with terror.

"We don't talk about mommy," Tom growls, trying to keep his voice low so I won't hear. It's a futile effort. I'm sitting less than a foot away, for Pete's sake. "I told you not to bring that up when daddy's around."

It's a Herculean struggle not to reach back and use Tom Craft's head for basketball practice. Who in the world talks to their child like that? Let alone a child who's been traumatized by the recent death of a parent? My dislike for Tom Craft grows with every new thing I learn about him. All the movie-star good looks in the world can't make up for a nasty interior. These children deserve far better.

I don't have to struggle for long, thankfully. I've had this route planned since Wednesday when I informed Brogan about my plan. I know I have only a few blocks before Tom Craft ceases to be my problem.

Serena stares bleakly out at the snow-laden landscape instead of at her father, biting her lip and wiping discreetly at her nose. I just want to pull her into my lap and hold her until all the hurt goes away. Even if Tom isn't our murderer, someone needs to do something for these kids.

When we round the corner onto Melrose Street, I see Brogan's squad car pulled off to one side, with the man in question kneeling by the wheel well of the vehicle. He appears to be struggling with the tire iron.

I bring Holly and Mistletoe to a stop beside him, and he winks discreetly up at me. All according to plan so far.

"You look like you're having a bit of trouble there, Chief. Need some help?"

"I could use some, yeah," he grunts, pushing on the tire iron for emphasis. "The darn thing seems to be rusted in. Could I get a hand, Tom?"

Tom eyes the chief, suspicion written all over the gorgeous planes of his face. "Suppose I say no?"

Brogan shrugs. "Carol will help me. Or maybe I could get your boy there to do it if his big, strong daddy isn't up for the challenge?"

A muscle in Tom's jaw tics in an unfairly attractive manner. He knows he's being baited and still can't help but rise to it anyway. He's too cocky to do much else.

"Yeah, fine. I can help you out, Chief."

He climbs out of the sleigh, and I start the horses forward again so the children and I are waiting for his return almost ten feet away. When I glance back, Brogan and Tom have bent over the tire again, talking in low murmurs.

The children and I sit in awkward silence for a minute

before I have the courage to speak to them. Even though it's my idea, this still feels morally suspect. After all, I'm about to ask these children about something deeply personal and possibly distressing. But if it helps to catch their mother's murderer, it has to be worth it in the end, doesn't it?

"It's been a rough week, huh?" I begin weakly. Talk about the understatement of the year. I truly hope these children never have a worse day in their lives.

Serena nods in agreement. Clark huffs. I raise a brow at him.

"What's that for?"

"I don't want to stay with daddy," he says softly. "He doesn't seem to care that mommy's gone. He won't let us talk about it, and he keeps bringing that other woman over. I don't like her. I want to go stay with grandma and grandpa."

Again, my heart aches for the pair of them. I shouldn't be talking about this. I can't make them any promises or give them anything to make the situation better. I'm half-hoping Tom is the murderer now, just so CPS will have to find a better place for these kids. If not, I'm afraid that Diane and Nina's unhappy pronouncements might hold true—they'll have an overbearing stepmom in a year or two.

"I'm sorry about what's happened." What else can I say?

"He doesn't care about us," Clark continues stubbornly. "He left us alone in our rooms that night. He came back late, and he was acting funny." He peeks up at me, blinking tears from his dark eyes. "Did my daddy hurt my mommy?"

I'm about to swallow my tongue at this news. This clue is more confirmation than I ever expected to get, especially as I've only begun looking into this for Brogan. I clear my throat, which has gone as dry as the Sahara.

"I really hope not, Clark," I whisper. "Police Chief Peterson will talk to him about it soon. Will that make you feel better?"

Clark nods and settles back into his seat. "Thank you for the ride, Ms. Green. This is nice."

I hand the cookies back to him, and he nibbles at one unenthusiastically. Still, the admission seems to have done him good, bringing some color back into his cheeks and returning some of his appetite. He shares his cookie with Serena, and they polish off two together before the shouting begins.

Tom Craft is cursing up a storm ten feet behind us, and I crane my neck to try to find the impetus for it. He pushes his face close to Brogan's, and he doesn't look the least bit appealing now. His eyes bulge, his face purples, and a vein pops visibly against the skin of his temple.

Conflicting desires war in me. The desire to slap my hands over the children's ears so they don't have to hear this and the desire to run to Brogan, installing myself as a soft wall between the pair of them.

Ultimately, Tom makes the decision for me, tossing the tire iron at Brogan's feet with another swear word, narrowly missing Brogan's toes. Snow flies up at the impact, and Tom storms toward the sleigh. He shoots me a poisonous glare before barking orders at his kids, biting out the words savagely in his anger.

"Clark. Serena. Get out of there now."

"But Mr. Craft—" I protest. "You're still ten blocks from home, and it's very cold. Let me—"

"Out!" he thunders, reaching over the side of the sleigh to pluck his forty-pound daughter from the bench seat. Clark scrambles out after her, not waiting to be snatched up as well. He stuffs the Ziploc bag of cookies I handed him into his pocket for safekeeping.

"Goodbye, Ms. Green," Clark mutters sullenly. If this turn of events shocks him, it doesn't show.

I grind my teeth. Something has to be done about Mr. Craft, and soon.

Tom Craft half-drags his children down the remainder of the block, whips around the corner, and disappears from sight.

I stare after him, gobsmacked, the desire to lob a nasty name at him strong.

Brogan sidles up to the side of my sleigh and props an elbow next to mine with a sigh. "I think I speak for both of us when I say that was a fiasco."

I nod emphatically. "I'm glad it didn't come to violence, though. What happened? Did you learn anything?"

"I was trying to be subtle, putting out feelers to see how he feels about the whole situation. I guess I tipped my hand by asking what he'd planned for New Year's."

I poorly hide a smirk and a roll of the eyes. Brogan and subtlety gel about as well as oil and water. It shouldn't surprise me that he's managed to antagonize the jumpy vet tech.

"What did he say?"

"That he was having dinner with Rose Fletcher at Foresters in Glovin County during the time the murder would have occurred. Says he can give me the name of the sitter and everything."

"That story is complete horse hockey. Clark said his father was gone for hours and that he forbade them from leaving their rooms until he got back. I didn't hear a mention of a babysitter at all. So someone's lying, and call me crazy, but I don't think it's the kid."

Brogan's eyes light up at this new information. "I can't admit the testimony in court, I'm afraid, but it might be enough to get me a warrant if I play my cards right. Great work, Carol."

I duck my head so he won't see I'm blushing, pleased by the praise. "Is your car going to recover from this little ruse?"

He chuckles. "It didn't turn out to be a ruse after all. I woke up to find the tire flat as a pancake this morning and barely managed to force it this far. I'm going to have to call a tow truck to get it to Dino's garage. I don't suppose I can bum a ride off you? I've got another lead I have to follow up on before I can go into the station today."

I pat the side of my bench seat. "Hop in. It's on the house."

He beams. "You're good people, Carol."

He gingerly moves Stockings to the backseat, only frowning down at her instead of plying her with his usual glower. Brogan is highly allergic to cats and will probably have sniffles after just this brief encounter. Still, he's gentle with her and even gives her ear a light scratch before settling in beside me.

"Where to?"

"Skye High Jewelry. Vaughn King thinks he might have a lead for us."

CHAPTER SEVEN

Vaughn King's eyes are red-rimmed behind his spectacles, and his nose is worn raw from too many Kleenex encounters. He hastily stuffs a tissue into a coat pocket as we enter Skye High Jewelry.

"Welcome to Skye High Jewelry. We're here to take your look out of this world. How can I help you folks today?"

He rattles off the stock line dutifully, though anyone with ears can tell there's no heart behind it.

Brogan offers the bereaved man a gentle smile, scuffing his boots on the welcome mat so he won't track in rock salt and slush from the sidewalk. I follow suit, coming through the door after Brogan.

Vaughn has swapped his usual slate-gray suit for a more somber black. In fact, the two workers in the shop are wearing black as well. Everyone has the somber attitude of a funeral-goer, which I suppose is apropos. It hasn't been all that long since Skye's death. She was the founder of this place, and it was her blood, sweat, and tears that made the shop what it is. These people have worked with her for years.

The sense of loss in the room is so potent, it almost chokes me.

There are only two occupants in the store at the moment; I'm surprised one of them isn't Mary. She's been catching flack for the incident with Bruno. Her boss, Marcy Gourd, isn't the most pleasant woman to work for, but she's grown on me. After being cleared of her brother's murder by yours truly, she'd warmed to us as well. It was she who sold his home to us for a steal last month.

We approach the glass case that doubles as a counter and checkout station. Brogan peers down at the case holding a lovely turquoise necklace and a dozen small studs glinting from silver settings. It's something Mary would like. We share the same birthstone, and even missed sharing a birthday by four hours. I was born Christmas Eve, and she on Christmas Day. I once again consider buying her a present.

Her grandmother would do it in a heartbeat. Just the thought of the crone makes my blood pressure skyrocket. I make it a habit not to hate anyone, but what I feel for Giles and Isla comes close. They stole my baby girl from me, raised her contrary to what I believe, and spoiled her to boot. She turned out well in the end, but it's no thanks to them. Heaven knows where she found the work ethic she has.

Even now, Isla likes to rub her wealth in my face, reminding me that she provides much better for Mary than I ever could.

Brogan beckons me forward, shaking me from my gloomy reverie, and I join him at the counter. He bends low on the pretext of examining the necklace more closely and pitches his voice low so only Vaughn and I can hear what's being said.

"You said you had a lead for us?"

Vaughn nods, sniffling. "I'm not sure if it's concrete, but I still thought you ought to know. It's happened again."

I glance between the two men, feeling as though I've missed something crucial.

Brogan's face creases into stern lines of disapproval. "I'm sorry, Vaughn, but investigating petty theft isn't high on my priority list right now. You should have called this in or cornered Dawson. I'm sort of busy trying to catch Skye's murderer. So if you don't have anything relevant to add to the case—"

"I do," Vaughn interjects. "I think the two are connected."

"I'm sorry to butt in, but what are you two talking about?" I say.

Brogan looks up from his contemplation of the glass and purses his lips, clearly trying to decide if it's worth divulging. I stare at him expectantly. He must have come to the conclusion that it is, because he elaborates in the same low whisper.

"Do you know Azalea Marshall?"

"Not personally, but I've heard of her. She's Nina Marshall's oldest, right?"

Brogan nods. "She's been reported multiple times in the past few years. She's been suspended twice for violent behavior, been to juvie once, and has most recently been reported in a string of thefts. If the items hadn't been returned, she would probably have been guilty of first-degree larceny. It's punishable with up to twenty years in jail if she's charged as an adult. But the thing is, no one has caught her at it. CCTV footage is inconclusive, and Vaughn can't seem to catch her. She's barred from the store for good, but it hasn't stopped the thefts."

He swings his gaze back to Vaughn. "But what does that have to do with the murder?"

"She snuck into town hall during Skye's meeting the day of the murder. They had a brief tussle. It was no more than a few shoves and name-calling, so we didn't think it was worth reporting. The more I think about it, though, I think it might have been more than that. She kept calling Skye a liar and told her she'd pay for what she'd done. I think she might have had something to do with it."

"But Skye was poisoned. How would she have even gotten her hands on the drugs that did it?" I asked.

Brogan chews his lip, deep in thought. "I think he may have a point, Carol. Azalea's father was in a car accident six months ago. He still has chronic pain from the injuries he sustained. It's entirely possible he was prescribed Tramadol for the pain. If his prescription was stolen and all the pills were crushed and put into the wine, that would be enough to produce the lethal drug interaction she had."

What he's saying makes sense on paper. Azalea is an angry little reprobate with a history of violence and everything to lose. She probably has access to the medication used to poison Skye. She could have easily slipped the wine to Skye somehow. An anonymous gift. Or perhaps addressed to her falsely by someone she trusted.

But it doesn't sit right with me. Somehow, I can't imagine Azalea Marshall poisoning Skye, no matter how much bad blood there was between them. She's so young, and the response seems so disproportionate. Tom Craft still seems like a more likely culprit.

"It seems a bit far-fetched," I say, trying to keep my tone level and polite. I don't want to offend Vaughn. He looks upset enough already. The idea that he's helping the investigation along seems to be bolstering him.

"Not as much as you'd probably think. She's been convicted several times. If she gets tried in court again, she's being charged as an adult. Twenty years of freedom gone, just like that. It might be enough to kill for," Brogan says.

Vaughn turns away from us, selecting a tray of diamonds from its position behind the counter. "Thank you for coming to speak with me, Chief. I'm afraid I've got to get back to work. These aren't going to set themselves, you know."

"Of course," Brogan agrees easily. "Give me a shout if you learn anymore."

"Will do."

Vaughn disappears into a back room. I watch him go, unsure of what to make of this new information. The case seems to be getting more complicated the longer we search. There are two official suspects now, maybe three. I can't discount Rose Fletcher, either. She and Tom had been up to something, and trained Bruno to snatch things. What exactly were the pair after?

I amble out into the crisp January air behind Brogan. I don't speak until we're back in the sleigh and on our way back to the police precinct. Brogan received a text sometime during our visit to inform him that his car should be ready in an hour or two, so at least I'm not going to be his only means of transportation all day.

"What do you think?" I ask.

"I don't know," Brogan admits. "It seems promising. And yet..."

And yet, it doesn't sit right with him, either.

"We could just ignore it," I say. "The police get bogus or well-meaning tips all the time, right?"

"I don't think we can discount it out of hand. Vaughn knew Skye better than anyone else, even her own husband. If he thinks Azalea might have something to do with it, I think it's at least worth investigating."

"It's your investigation, so it's your call. How do you want to proceed?"

"We'll do our due diligence," he decides after a second of thought. "We'll find her, ask her a few questions, try to get an alibi."

It sounds reasonable. Just a peaceful talk. So why is it still bothering me? I'm still left wondering when I drop Brogan off and am alone with my thoughts.

And even when I settle in at home that night, I still have no satisfactory answer.

UNTITLED

d

CHAPTER EIGHT

zalea Marshall is hard to pin down.

Even her mother, who I see on a semi-regular basis for sleigh rides, doesn't know where she is eighty percent of the time. Azalea does a variety of odd jobs for cash, seemingly has few friends, and never seems to stay in one place for long. She skulks home every now and then to eat or catch some shut-eye, but even that's sporadic. Azalea seems to be a small, unpredictable hurricane, and it makes me dizzy trying to track her path.

Which is why I'm half-convinced that our lead is a dud. Surely Azalea isn't at something so innocuous as a birthday party. But Brogan, Dawson, and I find ourselves in the lobby of the Pershing Ice Rink, located in our neighboring town. The town is only located about seven miles east of Tinsel Pine, which means it's technically inside Brogan's jurisdiction. Still, he seems a little uncomfortable being here.

Or maybe it's just the ice skates he's wobbling in. The things are a little too big for them, and they're ungainly. I don't blame him for his trepidation. Dawson grins from ear to ear, his big, boyish face lighting up as he makes his way awkwardly to the ice rink. He's younger than both of us, in his late twenties or mid-thirties.

"It's been so long since I've done this," he says, enthused. "Not since high school, at least."

"Glad someone's happy," I mutter, adopting a duck walk as I follow them both to the edge. Cold radiates off the sheet of ice in front of us. I shiver, despite my heavy coat with its down interior. Who wants to go skating in January? Isn't it cold enough already?

"No goofing off," Brogan snaps. "We locate Azalea, and we pull her aside. That's all we're doing."

Dawson reaches the edge of the rink. He gives us both a wink and a salute of acknowledgment before taking to the ice, moving as gracefully as a swan. A stab of envy twists in my chest. If only I could be so nimble. I'm pretty sure I'm going to fall on my well-padded behind and flop around on the ice like a beached seal. What an embarrassing spectacle that will be.

Brogan takes my hand in his broad calloused grip and looks down at me, apprehension melting away like a dusting of snow after rain, leaving a wisp of a smile in its place.

"If I go down, I'm taking you with me," he informs me in a light, conspiratorial tone.

"Ditto," I say with a grin.

We step out onto the ice at the same time, both of us windmilling forward as we try to lose our balance after the first few seconds. Brogan does manage to steady himself on the thick siding that encircles the rink. He stands me up straight, and we inch along the wall, keeping our eyes peeled for Azalea.

We find her in the middle, spinning in lazy, fluid circles. She looks similar to her mother. A pretty, heart-shaped face.

PERIL AND A PEPPERMINT PIG

Blond hair that hangs straight as a ruler, though hers has a tint of strawberry to it when the light hits it just right. Does she have the same big baby blues as her mother? She's too far away to tell.

I'm reluctant to push away from the safety of the wall. The very real fear of falling on my face is almost intolerable, but it looks like I'll have to. Azalea seems in no hurry to return to the edge of the rink. So I follow Brogan's lead, and we begin our slow, careful trek toward the middle. Dawson slides past us a few times. He could have already approached but is waiting for Brogan to spearhead our little investigation instead.

It takes us five minutes to get within speaking distance of the girl, and another two to get her to open her eyes and take notice of us.

She skids to a stop, staring at us. I suppose I have the answer to my question now. Azalea's eyes are precisely the same color as her mother's, but somehow even larger in her lean face. The girl looks like she's missed a few too many meals.

"Azalea Marshall?" Brogan inquires, trying to sound serious and professional. The effect is somewhat ruined by the ungainly wobble he performs. It shakes me as well, and I almost tumble backward onto my bottom. Dawson steadies me on the other side, and I shoot him a grateful smile.

"Yeah?" she says.

Brogan reaches beneath his heavy coat to retrieve his badge. "I'm Police Chief Brogan Peterson with Tinsel Pine PD. If you could just answer a few—"

He doesn't get to finish his sentence. The second she laid eyes on the badge, she was already in motion. She takes off, sliding quickly and gracefully toward the opposite end of the rink, leaving only a spray of ice in her wake.

Brogan snarls a swear word and tries to go after her, only succeeding in falling flat on his face. I, astonishingly, don't go down with him. I am yanked down, bending at the waist to keep ahold of his hand.

"Dawson!" Brogan barks.

"On it," the young man replies. He takes off after Azalea. He's still a few yards behind her, but he's closing the distance quickly.

I help Brogan to his feet unsteadily, and together, we make our way to the other wall of the rink. The second we're on solid ground again, Brogan yanks his skates off. I follow suit, though more slowly. Brogan doesn't even bother trying to retrieve his boots. He just starts running in socked feet, following the retreating forms of Dawson and beyond him, Azalea.

I slip on my snow boots and take off as well. Eyes track us all the way across the room. We must look like a gaggle of lunatics, chasing after a teenage girl. Again, I'm confronted by the fact that I need to be in shape because I'm nowhere close to catching up to Brogan. Huffing breaths in and out, I do my best to keep a steady pace and to ignore the giggles I can hear coming from a gaggle of kids near the door.

When I emerge into the crisp January air, I inhale a lungful of flurries. The snow has started again, coming down in thick globules. Blinking through the low visibility, I see I'm already too late to be of any help. Dawson and Brogan have Azalea pinned, pressed against the brick wall. Her cheek is bunched against the wall, and her voice comes out distorted when she tries to speak.

"I didn't do anything!" Azalea cries, thrashing uselessly as Dawson slaps cuffs onto her thin wrists. "I swear it! I'm not guilty."

The lady doth protest too much, in my opinion. She is

already trying to compose a defense against an accusation she hasn't even heard. Maybe Vaughn has a point after all.

I stare into the wide, frightened eyes of the girl, wondering if I'm staring into the eyes of a killer.

CHAPTER NINE

Azalea Marshall invoked her right to remain silent after being sequestered in Tinsel Pine PD's interrogation room. It is clear to everyone assembled that she's familiar with legal procedure. Familiar enough to wiggle out of this tight spot? None of us are sure yet. Her lawyer is running late, leaving Brogan and Azalea to stare frostily at each other across the worn surface of the interrogation room table.

I've never actually been inside the back rooms of the precinct. When I was detained on suspicion of murder last month, Brogan handcuffed me to the arm of an antique rocking chair while carrying out the line of questioning. He had nothing on me, really, and let me go shortly afterward. Since then, I've only slipped in once or twice to bring him coffee and a batch of my cinnamon cookies.

I stare around the room in avid interest. It looks almost exactly the way it's portrayed on TV. A table in the middle of the room. A bare bulb hanging overhead, casting a dim circle of light onto Brogan's and Azalea's heads. The walls are a gloomy gray, with only a small pane of one-way glass to break up the monotony. The equipment is a little worn, the finish wearing off the table and chairs in places.

When Azalea breaks the silence, it's so unexpected I actually jump. She turns her head to fix me with an unhappy stare and says, "What is *she* doing here?"

I've been wondering that as well, if I'm completely honest. There's no reason for me to be huddled in the corner watching the proceedings. I didn't contribute meaningfully to her capture. It's Vaughn's tip that brought Azalea in. I feel rather superfluous.

"She's my consultant," Brogan answers in a clipped tone. "And I don't think you're in any position to be picky, Azalea."

"Lea," she huffs. "Don't call me that. It's a stupid name."

"I think it's rather pretty," I offer in a conciliatory tone. Clearly, Brogan isn't destined to play anything but the bad cop.

Azalea's pretty pink mouth twists into a sneer. "I don't think I asked for your opinion, lady."

Brogan's brow is a mass of angry lines. He raps his knuckles angrily on the table. "You will keep a civil tongue in your head when you talk to her."

"You're not my freaking father," Azalea snaps back just as hotly.

Part of me is warmed by Brogan's defense of my honor. He's the nicest he's been in over a week today, and I don't want that to stop. But as someone who has a daughter and has witnessed teenage behavior often over the years, I know Brogan is doing himself no favors. The more he antagonizes her, the harder she'll dig her heels in.

"No, I'm not," Brogan agrees. "Because if I were, you'd have been sent to military school after the second account of stealing."

I can practically see Azalea's blue eyes frost over. Her

expression is wintery, her mouth set into a furious, white-lipped line.

"I don't have to take this from you," she says finally, then lapses back into silence, staring at the wall furthest from Brogan and me.

The silence doesn't last long, however. From outside the door, there comes a scuffing sound, a murmur of low voices, and then the scrape of the key in the lock. The door swings open seconds later to reveal two people in the gap. One, the familiar sight of Dawson. The other, a complete stranger.

He's a head shorter than me, which makes him the shortest person I've ever seen, excluding those with dwarfism. He's probably about five-four, with the thick heel of a dress shoe to boost him an extra inch. He's got more padding than I do, straining the buttons of his expensive three-piece suit with every puffing breath. His face is a perfect oval, the doughy skin threatening to overtake a prominent cleft chin. Beady black eyes are barely visible from behind thick tortoiseshell glasses. He's got a briefcase stuffed under one arm and a look of stern disapproval fixed on his face.

"Miss Marshall's lawyer is here," Dawson drawls unnecessarily. If his man is anything other than her lawyer, I'll eat his briefcase.

He stalks into the room and shoves his hand rather aggressively toward Brogan, staring him down until the chief takes it.

"I'm Joseph George, and I'm Miss Marshall's legal counsel."

I almost smile. Popular culture has taught me not to trust a man with two first names.

Brogan lets go of George's hand as soon as he possibly can, wiping a sheen of gleaming sweat onto his pants leg with a scowl.

"Have a seat, George. We've got a lot to talk about."

Joseph George unlatches his case and pulls out a manilla folder, placing it on the table with a thud. "On the contrary, Chief Peterson. I think there's very little to discuss here. You have nothing with which to charge my client."

"Oh, I don't? She resisted arrest. She's obstructing justice by withholding testimony."

"Trumped-up charges," George says with a dismissive wave of one pudgy hand. "No warrant was issued for her arrest. You had no suspicion of foul play with which to track her in the first place. I think a case could be made against *you,* Chief Peterson. You were clearly stalking my client."

I step forward, ready to restrain Brogan if he lunges for the rotund lawyer. He's leaning forward in his seat, teeth bared in a half-snarl.

"Don't you even start with that bull—"

"Brogan," I chide gently.

"Don't you 'Brogan' me, Carol. This little creep is trying to cite the law to me? To *me?"*

"It's just due diligence," I say quietly, trying desperately to diffuse the situation.

I don't think he'll actually take a swing at Joseph George, but there's no harm in being safe. It's been a hell of a month so far, so I can't blame him for being testy. There's so much on his plate. Another murderer on the loose, a meddling lawyer accusing him of wrongdoing, the press breathing down his neck, and my staunch refusal to sign his little relationship pact.

Brogan heaves in one furious breath, then two before he can get a handle on himself. His hands are still in white-knuckled fists when he turns back to Joseph George.

"We intended only to interview Miss Marshall, and she ran. Forgive me for thinking there was foul play involved."

"Well, I wasn't going to go down because that little rat-faced shopkeeper keeps lying about me," Azalea snaps. "I haven't done anything. The last time I did, it was October. You can ask my mother or my friends, but I haven't stolen anything."

"And even if she had," George interjects, "there's a precedent for dismissing the charges. You see, my client suffers from moderate to severe kleptomania."

Brogan snorted derisively. "Yeah, I've heard that one before."

Joseph rifles through his folder before producing a page. He slides it across the table to Brogan.

"You see here? This is a diagnosis from her psychiatrist." He produces another and slaps it down on top of the first. "Here is a list of appointments and medications she's had. I assure you, Miss Marshall's case has been documented thoroughly."

Azalea has dropped her gaze down to her lap, her cheeks flaming with embarrassment. She fidgets in her chair.

"I don't ever mean to do it," she mutters. "It just sort of...happens. I give everything back, honest. Even the stuff I took from Ms. Adams and Mr. King. It's about the act mostly, not the stuff. But Mr. King has reported me three times now, even though I haven't been in the shop since October. He's setting me up 'cause he's mad."

"And why would he do that?"

"'Cause he's a jerk," Azalea says sourly. "He and Ms. Skye both."

Brogan leans forward still further, pressing his advantage. "So, you admit you didn't like the deceased."

"Don't answer that," Joseph George cuts in automatically. "He's proceeding with a leading line of question. I advise you to wait and tell the police nothing. They have to press charges or release you."

Azalea ignores her lawyer, and that horrible sneering

expression twists her face again. "Yeah, I didn't like her. She lied about me."

"Is that why you killed her?"

Azalea recoils like he's slapped her. "Of course, I didn't kill her! I'm mentally ill, not a sicko."

"We've talked with your parents. You'd have access to the Tramadol that was used to kill the victim. You also had a confrontation with Ms. Adams on the day of her murder."

"Because she was lying about me!" she repeats, a note of desperation creeping into her voice now. "I went in there twice, okay? I didn't even steal the first time. I don't like the compulsion any more than you do. But it's there, okay? I give stuff back after I take it, and I don't go to places that will tempt me. Heck, I've even stopped going to the grocery store with Mom. I kept swiping the Juicy Fruit."

Brogan's expression is still supremely skeptical. Azalea's eyes narrow. She folds her arm over her chest, fingers digging into her biceps hard. It doesn't seem like a gesture of defiance to me, but more like she's closing herself off. She's not letting anything or anyone get close to her.

"I'm done talking to you," she whispers. "You're not going to give a crap about what I say, are you? You take one look at my record, and you write me off. Well, screw that. I'm not going to give you any fuel for your theories. Do you have anything to charge me with, Chief, or am I free to go?"

Brogan stews in silence for a minute and a half before cutting his head to the side in denial. Azalea gives him a chilly little smile.

"Great. Now let me out of here. I have a party to get back to."

CHAPTER TEN

The silence between us is loud as I drive Brogan home. We have to drive by the crime scene on our way back, which is sure to only worsen his mood. I can practically hear him composing a tirade meant for Joseph George.

After releasing Azalea back into her mother's custody, Brogan had locked himself in his office, speaking to no one. With no other rides planned for the day and nothing better to do with my time, I stayed in the precinct, tidying up and swapping pet stories with Dawson until the next shift rolled around. I offered Brogan a ride to his home, and he accepted.

And now here we are, physically close but mentally and emotionally miles apart. I sigh, reach into the pocket of my coat, and flick the white square of paper at Brogan. He jumps and glares down at it, uncomprehending.

"What's that?"

"Your relationship agreement. I signed it."

He blinks in surprise, and most of the anger drains away from his face. "You...what?"

"I signed the stupid thing. You needed something to go right, so here it is. I surrender. You win."

Brogan takes the page and unfolds it, examining my signature. He doesn't seem any happier, but at least he's not a pot about to boil over with rage now.

He traces the looping penmanship and frowns. "You don't have to say it like that."

"Like what?"

"Like I'm going to war with you. That was never my intent, Carol."

I loosen one hand from the reins and toss it skyward in frustration. "But that's all this has been, Brogan. You've been browbeating me to sign it since that day in the coffee shop. So I give up. You win. We'll do things your way."

His hands ball into fists on his lap. "Carol, be reasonable."

"I *am* reasonable. It's that document that's silly. You're asking me to sign a rigid schedule, a path with milestones that you get to set. Don't you see how silly it is? I'm fifty. You're going to turn forty-one soon. I've been unmarried for over two decades of my life, Brogan. I haven't dated anyone since the 1990s. Haven't been intimate with anyone for longer than that."

I watch his face from my periphery as we travel beneath the multi-colored streetlamps that dot Tinsel Pine's streets. They're pretty all year round, or so I'm told, but especially striking in winter, when the snow reflects the light back.

Brogan's hands clench and unclench, and his expression vacillates between frustration and guilt.

"It's the principle of the thing, Carol," he finally whispers. I almost don't hear him over the clip-clop of the horses' hooves on the lightly iced road. "You swear to do something, you should see it through."

I know he isn't talking about me now. I'm not sure

whether I want to hug him or shake him until his brain rattles around in his skull. Both seem appropriate. I've never met his ex-wife, but I hate her already. Brogan isn't a man who handles change well in the best of circumstances. For her to upend his world like this must be torture for him. She's broken something in the chief, and I'm not quite sure if anything but time can fix it.

"I can respect your boundaries, Brogan," I say quietly. "That's what communication is for. I don't have to sign an affidavit. I keep my promises. I'm not Sharona."

Brogan flinches at the mention of her name. Yes, I definitely hate her. He must have truly loved her for the reaction to be this visceral after half a year. His shoulders slump after a second.

"Yeah, I know."

That admission alone loosens the knot of compressed feelings in my chest. I realize now that at least part of my anger has been the idea that he doesn't differentiate. That he thinks I'm exactly the same as his two-timing ex-wife.

"You can't move on to anything healthy until you let go, Brogan."

He purses his lips. "You sound exactly like my therapist."

"Maybe he has a point."

Brogan chuckles weakly. "I wanted to believe he was a quack and that I was wasting two hundred an hour."

"It's not all mumbo-jumbo. Sometimes there's a kernel of wisdom in there somewhere. My point is, you're going to have to learn to trust me at some point."

Brogan peers down at the paper in his hands, and then nods to himself. He seizes both corners and rips the page clean in two. It's so unexpected that all I can do is stare.

"What are you doing?" I splutter. "I just signed it! Don't make me sign that thing again."

"I don't need this. You're right—I should trust you. I *do*

69

trust you. You're more reliable than anyone else in my life, except maybe Dawson."

My lips quirk up into a flirtatious smile. "And Dawson doesn't look half so pretty in a dress."

I smooth my red velvet dress for emphasis and primp my done-up curls in an exaggerated fashion.

Brogan actually gives a huge, rumbling belly laugh. "No, he does not. Saw him in drag once after he lost a bet. I will never let him live down the pantyhose and garter belt. The dress didn't look half bad, though."

The image that conjures makes me laugh, too. I need that picture to cheer me when days like these roll around. Our laughter dies after a minute or so, and he wipes at his eyes with a smile.

"The point is, I do trust you, Carol. You're right. This is probably silly, but thank you for the gesture. It means a lot to me."

I beam at his profile. With a half-smile on his face, he's astonishingly handsome. With all his hostility peeled off like a day-old face mask, he's an entirely different person. A person I want to know. A person I could possibly, someday, fall in love with.

I lean in and peck his cheek. I'll give him a more thorough kiss once we've reached his home. With any luck, he'll invite me in, and we can have a nightcap. Perhaps more, if I play my cards right.

At the very last second, Brogan turns his head, turning what should be an innocent kiss on the cheek into a full lip lock. His hands come up to cup the sides of my face at once, trapping my lips against his. I almost melt into him. His mouth is soft and a little chapped. The scent of his aftershave is like a jolt right to the libido. My grip on the reins slackens as I kiss back, the heat building between us.

The sleigh comes to a sudden, shuddering stop and the

sound of breaking wood fills the air. I pull away from Brogan at once, turning back in time to see the remnants of Skye Adams's mailbox split in two. The top half of the post and the metal mailbox plunge into the snow with a clatter. Holly and Mistletoe toss their heads with frantic whinnies.

Heat flushes into my face when I realize what I've done. In the seconds I was consumed in the kiss, the sleigh listed heavily to the right side of the road and managed to sideswipe Skye Adams's mailbox. I want to bury my face in my hands. *Stupid, stupid Carol.* I knew better. Both eyes on the road. Lustful driving is distracted driving, after all.

Brogan doesn't seem perturbed. If anything, he seems amused that he made me crash my sleigh. He climbs out and examines the damage to the side critically.

"It's just superficial damage," he says. "One coat of paint and you're good as new. However, I fear the Adams mailbox will never recover."

"Don't tease me, Brogan," I groan. "It's bad enough as it is."

I wait for his flippant reply, but it doesn't come. I raise my head, and I see he's staring at the Adams house. More specifically, at the severed police tape fluttering in the doorway and the broken door beyond it.

Someone was in the Adams house.

"Stay here," Brogan says grimly. "I'm going in."

CHAPTER ELEVEN

"**I**'m not leaving you alone," I hiss as he crunches his way through the yard, eyes fixed on the ruined doorway.

He barely turns back to look at me. "Oh yes you are, Carol. Someone has invaded my crime scene, and I doubt their intentions are good. So I want you to stay here and phone Dawson. I know you have him in your contacts. Some days, he won't shut up about the cat pictures and videos you send him."

I want to be flattered and amused by the fact that Dawson shares my texts with his curmudgeonly and cat-hating boss, but at this moment, I can't summon anything but panic. I can't let him walk into danger alone. We just reconciled, and there's so much still left to talk about.

I root around in my tote bag for my phone, scowling at Brogan's retreating back. He only directed me to call Dawson. He hasn't forbidden me from coming in after that's done.

I tap my foot impatiently as the phone dials. Dawson has an hour left on his shift. If I'm unlucky, he may have already clocked off, in which case I'll have to call the precinct and deal with Officer Terry, a veteran officer who doesn't like me much. Something about the fact that I'm dating his boss, I think. If I have to try to muddle through a conversation with him, the culprit may have already hurt Brogan.

Thankfully, Dawson picks up on the third ring. He sounds dead on his feet, and if this were anything less than an emergency, I would hang up and let the poor man catch some shut-eye at his desk.

"Hey, Ms. Green," he greets with a yawn. "What's going on? I was about to ask Terry if I could clock off early."

"Someone has broken into Skye Adams's home. Brogan is already inside, and he told me to call you and get backup."

Dawson sucks in a breath. He sounds more alert when he responds.

"I'll have a car over there in five. You and the chief hang tight, okay?"

He takes a cue from Brogan and doesn't say goodbye. I can forgive Dawson a pass on this one, though. Time is of the essence. And speaking of which...

I climb out of the bench seat at the front of the sleigh and loop Holly's and Mistletoe's reins around the Wallace family's mailbox, praying it's strong enough to hold them should they spook. Then I take off as fast as my legs will carry me, following the trail of Brogan's footprints to the front door.

The screen door has been taken entirely off its hinges, and the inner door has chunks missing. It appears to have been beaten in by something or someone. I have to dance over a field of wood splinters threatening to stab at my ankles. When a shape moves in the gloom just in front of me, I release a squeak a mouse would be proud of and duck, shielding my head with my hands.

I swear the shape growls at me.

"What did I tell you, Carol?" Brogan snaps at me. "Get out of here."

Relief knocks the wind from me. It's just Brogan moving inside the living room, probably groping for a light.

"And I told *you* that I wasn't leaving you alone. What if you came in here and got stabbed? I couldn't keep my thumb plugged firmly up my behind while you wade into danger."

"If I get stabbed, you're right behind me. I think one of us should stay whole and healthy, don't you? That way, someone is up for calling 911?"

Well, when he puts it that way, it makes a certain amount of sense. I don't budge, though.

"You said you trusted me. Do you mean it?"

Brogan's face—what I can see of it from the diffuse, barely-there light from the window—creases in consternation. "Carol, it's not the same thing."

"Trust me to have your back," I insist.

He heaves a sigh and shakes his head, muttering that he must be insane, but he waves me forward. Together, we creep forward, careful to make as little noise as possible. The house shifts and creaks, settling like most old houses tend to do. It doesn't stop me from jumping at every small sound, eyes darting to find the source of the noise.

I step past the hall that leads to Skye's bedroom and her guest room, and something hurtles out of the dark toward me. I backpedal as hard as I can, but it's not quite enough. Something heavy collides with my shoulder so hard that it goes numb. My momentum launches me backward, and I hit the wall with a crunch of breaking drywall.

Brogan has found a light switch and flicked it on. The sudden illumination stabs mercilessly into my eyes. Fortunately, it also seems to take my attacker off-guard as well, because the next blow doesn't hit the side of my head and impacts the wall beside me instead.

A terrified shriek rips its way from my throat and I duck, instinctively raising my hands to shield my head. The pain slowly begins to trickle into my shoulder, and the throb is so fierce that I want to cry.

"Get out!" a hysterical female voice shrieks. "Get out, get out! You're ruining everything!"

Something heavy impacts the wall and shards of paint fall to the carpeted floor. Dust chokes me. I can't see my attacker clearly through the haze of tears in my eyes.

I expect the next blow to crack my skull open like a piñata. It doesn't come. I blink the tears from my eyes, daring to relax my crossed arms enough to peer through them at my attacker and what has stopped her attack.

Rose Fletcher stands stock still, her hands still gripped tight around the handle of an aluminum bat, intense fury shining in her eyes. Brogan stands at her shoulder, gun hovering close to her head. His unspoken message is clear. Move, and I shoot.

"Put the bat on the floor slowly," Brogan directs in a calm, even tone. I can't fathom how he's not shouting at her. The screaming panic that's been clawing at the base of my skull would render me incoherent.

Rose Fletcher looks as though she might refuse, her grip tightening on the handle. But then the tension goes out of her muscles, and she lets the bat swing to her side and land on the carpet with a heavy thud.

"Now lace your hands behind your back," Brogan orders. "Rose Fletcher, you are under arrest for second-degree battery, trespass, and evidence tampering. You have the right to remain silent. Anything you say can and will be used against you in a court of law. You have the right to an attorney. If you cannot afford an attorney, one will be provided for you."

Rose Fletcher continues to glare at me. I can't seem to

meet her eyes for long. The tremors start near my toes and quiver up the rest of me until even my teeth are chattering. For the first time in the evening, I feel truly frozen. I don't see remorse in her dark eyes, just a sort of frenzied determination. Her mahogany hair has come loose from its careful styling, adding to the overall impression that she's unhinged.

She just tried to kill me. That fact sinks in slowly. She'd been ready to kill someone she barely knew for reasons unknown. If she could do something like that to me, there was no doubt in my mind that she could have done it to Skye. She has the world to gain from it.

My theories flip on their head in the wake of this new information. She's been conspiring with Tom to do something. And now she's come back to erase the evidence of the crime.

I think Rose Fletcher may be our murderer.

Brogan pushes Rose firmly toward the front door, casting a worried glance my way. "Are you alright? I heard her land a hit before the lights came on. Are you concussed? Any broken bones?"

"Just a bruise, I think," I say, rubbing my shoulder, rotating the joint to try to alleviate some of the pain. It helps just a little. I let out a shaky little laugh, the sound hovering just on the verge of a sob. If I don't laugh, I will break down and cry. "I suppose this is where you say I told you so."

Blue and red light spirals through the night, and Dawson and Terry sprint toward the front door. Brogan shoves Rose in their direction, crossing over to me, sliding an arm around my waist so we can hobble out of the house together.

"Not a chance," he whispers. "Not after I came so close to losing you."

Then he kisses me. A chaste press of lips, but a welcome one. It warms me, making me feel treasured and loved. I'm not sure how to define what we have, but it's special. And for just an instant, it erases the aches in my body, the uncertainty of the future.

For a moment, we just stare at each other in a perfect moment of understanding. Then Rose starts yelling obscenities at Terry, and the spell is broken.

We step apart as reality settles back over us. There's still a murder to solve and my horses to tend to. So we part ways, with the promise we'll see each other again at the precinct.

The shakes resume when Brogan's gone, and don't go away until I'm walking through the front door of the precinct.

Rose Fletcher tried to kill me. I owe Brogan big time. When this investigation is over, I'm baking him a lifetime's worth of cinnamon cookies.

CHAPTER TWELVE

Dawson stands beside me like a solemn, silent sentry. I have the sneaking suspicion he's got orders from Brogan to watch me and make sure I don't keel over or something.

I must look more pitiful than I imagine because Brogan doesn't argue when I insist on being present at Rose's questioning. I half expected the big bear of a man to try to wrap me in cotton and stuff me away in a closet somewhere for safekeeping, not to emerge again until this investigation is over. It is gratifying to know that he's taking his promise seriously. By allowing me to be here, he's showing that he trusts me not to do something stupid. Again.

I stare through the pane of glass that looks in on the interrogation room. Even though Rose is safely cuffed to a chair and can't hurt me, I'm still twitchy. In all my years, I've never come so close to actually being hurt or killed. It's a sobering experience—one I don't plan to tell Mary about for some time. She'll already be frantic because I've ignored her last three voicemails. No need to add the case of near-lethal battery to her long list of worries.

"Do you need a coat?" Dawson asks in an undertone.

"Huh?"

"Do you need a coat?" he repeats. "You're still shaking a little."

Ah. So I am. It's nothing like the shakes I had at the house, but they're still there. I try to get a handle on myself. I've discovered two bodies in the last month and a half. I've been bowled over by massive dogs, chased thieving teens, and incapacitated a mailbox. It's just another thing on the laundry list of unfortunate happenings in Tinsel Pine. So I should calm myself down.

My focus shifts back to the task at hand when Brogan's voice filters through the crackling PA system on this side of the glass. I can only see his profile as he stares down Rose Fletcher, but it's still a sight to behold. I don't think I've seen him look this stony in the entire time I've known him. He practically radiates righteous indignation.

"Start talking, Fletcher," he says, tone taut with dislike. "Or I'm going to throw the book at you. What you did could be construed as attempted murder. There's a serious penalty for that. So if you want to avoid spending the rest of your life rotting in a jail cell, you better start cooperating, and you do it fast."

Rose has had time to arrange her mahogany hair to something more presentable since arriving. The hostility has drained from her face, leaving only blank apathy in its place.

"I wasn't trying to kill her," she says shortly. "I was trying to scare her. I wanted her gone."

It hadn't felt like that to me. The answer doesn't seem to please Brogan, either.

"Excuse me for saying it, Miss Fletcher, but that's complete and utter bull. You were in that house for a reason, and I believe you were willing to kill to cover it up. What were you trying to hide? Your involvement in Skye's murder, perhaps?"

Rose snaps to attention, drawing herself up to her full height. "Now who's tossing around cockamamie stories, Chief? I didn't kill Skye."

"Oh?" Brogan says, tapping his chin in an exaggerated manner, eyes narrowing on Rose. "Because from where I'm sitting, you had a stellar motivation. You had an affair with Skye's husband, and he didn't want to marry you until all the paperwork was done. I'm pretty sure you tried to guarantee your lover custody by default. Or maybe you were just jealous that he still talked with her."

"I didn't need to kill Skye," Rose sneers. "He wasn't hers anymore. Hadn't been for a long time. He left her for me, you know. Why would I be jealous of a woman who is too pathetic to hang onto her own husband?"

My anger and fear curdle in my stomach, and I feel a little sick. I've always hated women like Rose. Women who got a thrill from making married men stray. It's almost never about the man. It's about exerting power over the woman, proving you're desirable enough to take something from her.

"Charming, isn't she?" I mutter to Dawson. "I can *totally* see the appeal. All the charm and tenderness of a cactus."

Dawson, who'd been in the midst of slurping coffee from his mug, snorts into the liquid, splattering us both with warm espresso.

Brogan continues, oblivious to our commentary. "So, it sounds like you didn't think much of the victim."

Rose rolls her eyes. "Stellar powers of observation there, Chief. Of course, I didn't like her. She was a prissy little perfectionist who micromanaged everything. I even heard she was fighting with Vaughn King her last day alive, and you know how much that man loved to kiss her boots. It doesn't mean I killed Skye. I wasn't anywhere near her house on the day of the murder."

"That's not germane to the topic, Rose. You see, I don't really believe that you had nothing to do with this. Because when you were brought in, and your possessions were sorted through, we found this in your purse."

Brogan withdraws a plastic baggie seemingly from nowhere and drops it onto the table in front of him. I can barely see what's inside it from my vantage point. It looks like a scrap of paper.

"A receipt?" Rose asks, brow scrunching as she stares down at the slip. "So?"

"This is a receipt for Casine Blanc. You bought two bottles on December 31st. I'm willing to bet that at least one of them will match the one we have in evidence. The one you used to poison Skye."

Rose's expression flickers from apathetic to apoplectic in an instant. Her creamy skin flushes to the pink of an undercooked steak and tendons stand out in her neck. Now this looks more like the woman who attacked me. I don't even try to protest when Dawson shrugs off his coat and drapes it over my shoulders. It's not really the cold that's bothering me, but his gallantry soothes the edges of my nerves. These are all good men at Tinsel Pine PD, and none of them—even grumpy Terry—will let me be hurt. I have to believe that.

"That's not possible!" she shouts, slapping the table for emphasis. "I'm being framed! My card was stolen three days before Skye died! It was only just recently found in James Nelson's store."

Brogan's skepticism is etched deeply into the lines of his face. Even I, with my less-than-fabulous track record in judging people, can smell a lie that obvious.

"If you didn't make the purchase, why is the receipt still

in your purse, Rose?" Brogan drawls. "See, I think you did buy that wine. I think you forgot about the receipt that could be linked back to you. I think you thought you were pretty confident you could get away with it."

"Someone must have put it there! I didn't kill her! I hated her guts, but I didn't kill her! You have to believe me." Rose jerks at the cuff connecting her to the chair. It slides about a few inches. She jerks her head toward the door, the desperation of a caged animal on her face. She wants out of that room badly.

"Can she force the door?" I whisper to Dawson.

He shakes his head. "Locked. She's not going anywhere."

Brogan continues on ruthlessly, ignoring Rose's panic. "Want to know what I think, Rose? I think it was a joint effort. You got the wine, he got the Tramadol from the clinic. Together, you got rid of the one person standing in the way of your happily ever after."

"I didn't!" Rose gasps. "I didn't, I didn't, I didn't..."

Her face slips from pink to red, red to purple, and alarm bells start going off in my head when her lips turn blue. Her pupils are mere pinpricks, her breathing ragged. I have a sick feeling that this is not just a panic attack.

I jab my finger on the intercom button just as Brogan begins to rise to his feet.

"Call an ambulance, Brogan. I think she's been poisoned."

"Poisoned?" Rose echoes at a shriek. "You poisoned me?"

"Sit down and breathe, Miss Fletcher," Brogan snaps, psychologically incapable of switching gears to concern so quickly. "We didn't poison you."

But someone has. Because just a few seconds later, Rose's eyes roll back into her head and her body slumps toward the ground. She's saved from cracking her skull on the ground by Brogan's quick reflexes. He cradles the small, spindly woman between his large biceps and casts a glance back at the pair of us behind the glass.

Drat. Drat and more drat. Just when we think we have the culprit, another wrench gets thrown into the works. Rose Fletcher isn't a killer. She's another victim.

And now, we have to find the culprit who wants both of them gone.

CHAPTER THIRTEEN

"It wasn't Tramadol?" Marcy echoes, cocking a perfectly plucked brow to punctuate her incredulity.

Marcy Gourd is a slim brunette with only a few streaks of gray shooting through at her temples. We're not so far apart in age, and she doesn't look a day of it. I'm frankly a little envious of her seeming agelessness, especially now when I look as bruised as an overturned cart of apples. The number Rose Fletcher did on me is really beginning to show now, a day out from the attack.

Mary flanks her boss on the other side and is glaring accusations at me from across the booth at the Curds and Whey Diner, the home for the best cheese curds east of Wisconsin. I try to avoid her piercing gaze as much as I can. She's angry with me for leaving her out of this investigation, and I understand why. Skye was her friend, and I'm her mother. Obviously, the goings-on concern her. But she doesn't have to look so wounded. It's not as if I'm being malicious. I'm a consultant on an active police investigation, and there are some details I can't divulge.

This one, though, is pointless to keep to myself. Everyone

in Tinsel Pine has heard of Rose Fletcher's arrest and poisoning by now. Wild rumors circulate about how it happened, and if the police department has something to do with it. I might as well clear the air right here and now.

"No," I sigh, plucking a cheese curd roughly the size of a silver dollar from my basket. The rice paper barrier they've been placed on crinkles mournfully as I abscond with more of its cargo. "It wasn't. It was strychnine."

"Rat poison?" Mary asks, unable to help herself. "How did she ingest rat poison? Wouldn't you taste that?"

"Not necessarily. And it can be inhaled, too, which is what the doctors are guessing happened."

"Poor Rose..." Marcy mutters. "What a thing to happen. I'm just happy she's going to make a recovery. The doctors say she'll pull through, right?"

I nod, popping the curd into my mouth to keep myself from commenting. I'm not feeling particularly charitable after almost being beaten to death. I don't want Rose Fletcher to die, but an extended stay in the hospital, preferably under guard, would ease my mind.

"Do you think she faked it?" Mary asks. "I mean, the evidence against her was pretty damning. Maybe she's trying to throw the police off the trail."

"And poison herself? I don't know. That seems like a risky move."

I pick at the edge of a hangnail. The thought has occurred to me, of course. I'm not convinced that Rose has anything to do with it. The most recent poisoning shifts the suspicion still more firmly onto Tom. He has connections to both victims and a reason to want both of them dead. The local gossip mill says Rose has been leaning pretty heavily on him to produce a ring. Maybe he's gotten tired of her and decided to do away with her permanently.

If she were conscious, I'd visit her in her hospital and

grill her for answers. So much of this mystery still doesn't make sense. Tom and Rose have trained Bruno to snatch things. They pointed him in Skye's direction, but the dog didn't perform as expected, snatching a candied pig instead of whatever valuables they'd been after.

And how does Azalea Marshall fit into all of this? She's clearly scared of something and knows more than she's letting on.

Mary snaps her fingers in front of my face, and I blink back to reality. "What?"

"I asked you whether Brogan's got any theories. Where'd your brain go, Mom?"

"Gallivanting off without me no doubt," I say, taking a deep draft of bubbly diet soda. After the salty cheese curds, it feels like heaven. "And no, we're fresh out of theories at the moment. Brogan's going to get a warrant to search Tom Craft's house. Azalea Marshall has disappeared again, and he doesn't have anything to charge her with, in any case."

If I can locate the moody teen, maybe I can press her for answers. I can't put my finger on why, but I have the nagging feeling that she's a part of this, though I don't know how just yet.

We spend the hour between my appointments talking in circles, ultimately just rehashing the same tired points. When I leave to take my four o'clock for a ride around Tinsel Pine, I'm still preoccupied. I probably come across as terse to the pair of lovebirds canoodling in the back, because I only give yes or no answers to the few questions they ask.

When my work is finally done and the horses secured in their stable, I just amble around Tinsel Pine, still trying to parse out the truth. It's too cold to stay out long, but I make almost a complete circuit of the town before I'm willing to turn back. I'm passing the Tinsel Pine elementary and high school buildings when I spot a shape moving in the fenced-in playground.

It's a girl. A very familiar girl.

Silvery moonlight lines her ruler-straight blonde hair. I blink a few times, sure that my eyes are playing tricks on me. Surely not. Surely the girl I've been preoccupied with all day isn't right in front of me.

But when I look, she's still there. She's sitting stationary on a swing, scuffing the worn track beneath it with her tennis shoe. I amble over to the fence that screens the place in and find that the padlock that keeps it shut is hanging loosely. Pushing it aside, I stride onto the field. Most of the playground has been covered with Astroturf, with the exception of the swings and slides. My steps make almost no noise as I cross over to the preoccupied teen. I stop about three feet away from her.

"I think this is technically trespassing," I muse.

Azalea jerks in surprise and hops off the swing at once. She backs away from me, eyes hard and suspicious.

"You followed me here," she accuses.

"I was just walking by, actually."

"Liar," she sneers. "I know you're working for that cop. This is stalking. My mom's lawyer will come after you."

I lift a brow at her. "I think he'll have a hard time defending you since you were caught in the midst of a crime. I just want to talk, Lea. Sit down and have a chat with me, and I won't tell Brogan. I give you my word."

"Why should I trust you? I heard what happened to Rose Fletcher. I know you all tried to shut her up."

Her chin quivers just a little, though she's trying to look brave, which just guts me. Mary does that sometimes during soaps when one of her favorite characters dies.

Azalea is frightened of me. Honest-to-goodness terrified. Of me.

"That wasn't us, Lea. I swear that you don't have anything to fear from me. I just want to talk. Sit down, please."

I make the first move, sitting in the swing next to the one she vacated. The flexible plastic seat sags a little beneath my weight. I smile encouragingly and pat the seat of the swing next to me.

"Sit. Just five minutes, and I'll be out of your hair, promise. Or I could give you a ride back home if you like."

Azalea hesitates, eyes flicking between me and the open gate. If she decides to run, there's no way I can outpace her. I was never fast, even in the spry days of my youth. In the end, though, she sits and stares blankly ahead without once looking at me.

"What do you want to talk about?"

"That day at the ice rink, you ran. Why? We were just there to talk."

Azalea snorts. "Yeah, right. Cops are never there to 'just talk.' Oh, they like to talk *at* you, but never *to* you. You have anything close to a record, they don't even see you. They just see a rap sheet with a face attached."

I flinch because her description isn't entirely inaccurate. I've talked to my share of cops in the day, and Brogan and Dawson are the only ones I've ever trusted.

"I understand that, you know."

She rolls her eyes and makes another sound of derision. "Yeah, white-bread granny with her nice house and cop boyfriend feels my pain. What a load."

"I'm not a grandmother, and don't write me off just yet. I'll have you know that I've been arrested seven times. Eight, if you count last month, though I didn't get dragged in that time."

She finally turns a little in her seat to regard me with disbelief. "You're lying."

"I swear on my mother's grave. I was quite the upstart in college. My ex-husband and I took part in the Berkeley protests."

Her lips quirk rebelliously, though the rest of her face doesn't betray her amusement. "So what? That doesn't mean you have any insight into my life."

"I think I do," I say slowly. "I think you were afraid Brogan was there to charge you with something. One more offense and you go to jail, right?"

She nods. "It's not fair. The last several charges were bogus. I wasn't in Skye High Jewelry more than once."

"Why did you steal from them in the first place? You had to know it was going to get you in trouble."

Azalea stares at her pale hands, clenched into fists on her lap.

"It's not something I can really control. It's hard to describe it, too." She considers for a moment. "Have you ever had chickenpox, Ms. Green?"

"When I was a little girl. What's that have to do with anything?"

"That's what it feels like for me. An itch. It starts out small, just a little urge. The more I ignore it, the worse the urge gets, until it feels painful to *not* itch. And then, you start itching without meaning to. Sometimes you wake up and realize you've itched in your sleep. There's relief when you finally scratch the itch. It doesn't go away completely, but it stops the compulsion, at least for a little while. I can go a week or two without stealing, but eventually, it happens again, and again, and again. I tend to steal every day or two, just little things, to keep the urge low. Candy, nail polish, sunglasses. Stuff people tend to overlook. I took one of Skye's pigs that day, you know. Skye was livid. She called my mom, screaming that she was going to report me. I thought you guys might know and think that I murdered her to shut her up."

My chest feels tight, and my heart throbs with sympathy for the poor girl. Compulsions are a powerful thing, and there doesn't seem to be much that Azalea can do to master hers. She probably can't hold down a job, can't keep friends for long, and she's going to end up in jail sooner or later if nothing is done.

A stroke of inspiration hits me, and I swivel to face her, a big grin plastered all over my face. "Come work for me."

"What?"

"I said come work for me, Lea. You need a steady job, and I could use an assistant. I'll stuff my tote bag and the back of the sleigh with things you can find and steal. So long as you return them to me at the end of the day, I won't be angry. I'll give you half of what I make every sleigh ride."

She glances askance at me. "You're serious? 'Cause I don't appreciate it if this is a joke."

"No joke," I swear. "I want you as my assistant. The question is, do you want the job?"

"I do," she confesses. "I really do. You promise this isn't a trick to get me back in the station?"

"I promise."

Her lips curl into a phantom smile. "Alright, then. Any other rules?"

I consider it. "Don't steal my cat."

Azalea laughs. "Deal."

CHAPTER FOURTEEN

O ak Creek Hospital is an austere building, built at the turn of the century. Its stone walls carry all the stern disapproval of a matron, and I feel somehow guilty, even walking in its shadow. I pity the poor souls who have to live for any length of time within its walls.

The hospital is situated in the middle of a sleepy town in Glovin County. I escaped coming here by the skin of my teeth the night Rose attacked me. However, Rose Fletcher has not been so lucky, barely escaping the attempt on her life. The doctors say she may be able to make a full recovery, but she'll be laid out for at least a week.

The halls leading to her hospital room are pristine white, the staff bustling through them with brisk efficiency. Brogan and I opt to take the stairs to the fourth floor because I need the exercise, and he's humoring me. My muscles ache, reminding me that we're about to visit the woman who brutally assaulted me not so long ago. The shakes are back. I really don't want to see her, but it's necessary. She's awake and responding, so we need to question her.

"You don't have to do this, Carol," Brogan says, voice

almost as gentle. Or at least as gentle as this gruff man can manage. "If you're scared, you can wait in the car."

I stand up a little straighter and grip the stair railing a little harder. It's never been in my nature to be cowardly. I lived on the road for years, traveled to exotic locales, tackled every adventure that I could find. I can face one woman.

"I'm fine."

Brogan sighs. "If you insist."

We emerge onto the fourth floor a few minutes later, and he stops before the receptionist's desk to ask which room we'll find Rose in. The receptionist directs us to room 4036.

A lone security guard is positioned outside her door. He's a blond, balding, middle-aged man who can barely squeeze into his uniform. He looks sleepy, but he stands a little straighter when he spots our approach. He inclines his head respectfully to Brogan.

"Sir."

Brogan nods back, and the man returns to his slouch. I'm not sure whether he's here to keep anyone from hurting Rose or to keep Rose from hurting other people. Both, if I had to put money on it.

Rose's eyes are a little glassy and fixed on a television screen mounted in the upper right-hand corner of the room. It looks like reruns of a sitcom. She's smiling faintly, and it's the friendliest expression I've seen on her face to date. It drops off her face like a stone when she turns to look at us. The lines around her eyes tighten as she stares Brogan down.

"Come to finish what you started?" she hisses.

"You and I both know you were dosed before you ever set foot in my precinct, Miss Fletcher," Brogan replies. "I want to figure out who did it as much as you do. I can't do that unless you cooperate with me. Where were you before you broke into the Adams house? Who were you with?"

Rose crosses her arms over her chest and lifts her chin in

a move I think is supposed to look defiant. Instead, it looks a little pitiful. She's yet to regain her color, and bruise-like shadows bloom beneath her eyes. She's thin, drowning in the paisley material of her hospital gown. It's hard to believe this is the same woman who came after me with a bat.

"I don't have to talk to you."

"That's true," Brogan acknowledges with a nod. "And you can request a lawyer if you want. But I don't think you did this, Rose. Not anymore. Someone tried to kill you and I want to figure out who. If you cooperate, I think I can make a case to a judge to wave the charges for trespass. And you'll get probation for the assault."

Rose's face twitches as she struggles not to express interest. "How many years?"

"Five, and we'll waive the fee as well. Does that sound acceptable to you?"

Rose pretends to consider it, but I can see her answer in her eyes long before she speaks. This is the best deal she will get, and she knows it.

"Fine. What do you want to know first?"

"Why you trained Bruno to steal small objects," I interject before Brogan can open his mouth to repeat his questions. "I heard you and Tom the other day at the Four Legacy Clinic. He convinced you to train Bruno to steal. Do you know why? What was he after?"

Rose shrugs. "He kept telling me he just wanted to mess with Skye. Steal some of her papers, disrupt her meetings, make her look bad in front of the investors. I know it's not the whole story. Bruno ended up snatching one of those stupid candy pigs she was selling instead, and he ended up losing it in the halls anyway. We came away with nothing to show for it. Tom was livid."

My lip curls. How petty could one man get? The man was a candy-coated rat pellet. Appealing on the outside, but with an awful center. No wonder Skye had been divorcing him. Once again, I pity his poor kids.

Brogan shoots me a suspicious glance. "You never told me about that."

It's my turn to shrug. "I didn't think it was relevant at the time. Just a silly prank. Do you think it might be more?"

"Possibly, but it doesn't answer my question," he says, turning back to Rose. "What were you doing at the Adams house in the first place?"

"Searching for answers. Tom wasn't telling me something, and I know it had something to do with *her*. I wanted to know what secrets he was keeping from me."

Brogan seems to take that at face value, writing it down on the small pad of paper he keeps in his uniform pocket.

"Where were you, and who did you see on the day of your poisoning?"

Rose's cute little nose scrunches as she struggles to come up with her answer.

"Work, mostly. And then I went to Tom's house. He sent the kids to their grandparents for the night. We were going to have a romantic dinner, but the place was a mess because the kids had been playing. He and I cleaned the house and...he spilled Borax all over me. At least, I thought it was Borax."

Her eyes fly open wide, the realization smacking her in the face hard. The poor girl actually looks surprised, as though she's just now realizing the monster she's been dating.

"He poisoned me! How could he? We're in love!"

"*You* were in love," I correct sadly. "He was just in it for a good time. You weren't fun anymore—you were a liability who knew too much. He had to get rid of you."

Her eyes well up with shiny tears. "I don't understand. He said he'd leave her to be with me. Why would he...?"

She cuts off with a choked sound and ducks her head so we won't see the tears that spill down her face. "He can't have. He loves me. He loves me. He loves me..."

Rose keeps repeating that litany, even as we walk out the door. It's still ringing in my ears, even as we exit the hospital.

Love can pardon a multitude of sins. But can it really forgive attempted murder?

Somehow, I don't think so.

CHAPTER FIFTEEN

The Four Legacy Animal Clinic's parking lot is close to empty near closing time. Brogan has secured a warrant for Tom Craft's arrest, arrangements have been made to take his children into protective custody until a social worker can arrive, and Rose has been placed under heavier guard in case Tom tries something again.

"I gotta admit, the Borax thing was clever," Brogan says in an undertone as we approach the front door of the clinic. "Easy to play off as an accident, and she never suspected anything until it was too late."

"You almost sound like you admire him," I hiss back.

"I don't. I'm just saying that it's clever. It makes me wonder why he tried something as obvious as dosing a wine bottle with his ex-wife. And why would she drink anything he gave her? She had to know how ticked he was about the custody battle. I wouldn't trust a thing my wife gives me."

I jerk a little at the mention of his wife. Given how much animosity Brogan clearly has toward her, it's shocking to remember that he's technically still married. The proceedings won't be final until next month, at the very earliest. I flush a little around the collar, suddenly feeling like a hussy. I'm dating a married man.

"That's assuming she knew it was from Tom," I point out. "It could have been passed along by someone else. Or dropped off anonymously."

"True. But it still bugs me."

"He's the most likely culprit," I point out. "He tried to kill Rose, and he probably killed Skye, too, just so he could keep his kids."

"Maybe."

Brogan grips the handle and swings the door wide, gesturing for me to enter. I step inside quickly, once more buffeted by that distinctly animal odor that clings to the clinic like musk.

The lobby is empty but for Helen and Tom, who are deep in conversation. Tom has his elbow propped on the counter, an enticing smile plastered onto his handsome face. Helen is a little pink in the cheeks and is hiding a smile of her own, fiddling with a lock of her dirty-blond hair, winding it round and round one finger.

That low-down jerk. He's flirting with another woman after poisoning the two that came before her. I want to push poor, unsuspecting Helen out the clinic door and take a bat to the man. How vile.

Both of them look up as we enter, conversation ceasing immediately.

"We're closing in ten minutes," Tom says shortly. "You can come back tomorrow."

Helen pats Tom's arm with a disarming smile. "It's alright, Tommy. We've got just a little time. Is Stockings okay, Ms. Green?"

She bends to peer into my tote bag expectantly, searching for my cat's fuzzy head. She finds only my wallet and sundry supplies inside.

"Stockings is fine," I assure her. "We're here to speak to Tom."

"About what?" he says, eyes flashing with sudden pique. "The little ambush you set up for me the other day? I'm still waiting for an apology for that, by the way."

"I'll do you one better," Brogan says with an unpleasant smile. He draws a piece of paper from his back pocket. "This is a warrant for your arrest, Tom. You're being charged with the attempted murder of Rose Fletcher and the murder of Skye Adams."

Tom bolts. He bangs through the door to the back so fast that I'm left staring blankly at the spot he vacated for a second or two. Brogan is after him in an instant, taking off like The Flash, disappearing into the back as well. Behind as always, I don't get my stubby legs going until both men are out of sight.

I enter the narrow corridor just in time to witness first Tom, then Brogan round a corner toward the room where the kennels are kept. The baying of dogs signals their passage through.

I'm already huffing with exertion when I reach the doorway. Brogan is being waylaid by dogs. Beagles, Corgis, Dalmatians, and a few tiny Yorkies swarm around his ankles hopping, howling, and yipping with joy at their sudden freedom.

There are cats free as well, slinking away from the dogs as quickly as they can without drawing their notice. Brogan is sneezing up a storm, tears streaming from his eyes.

"Get these things off me!" he yells over the din.

Helen has appeared behind me, and she lets out a sharp whistle, which turns the head of every dog in the room. A glance back shows she's holding an enormous bag of dog treats. She unseals it and plucks a treat shaped like a squiggly bacon strip, waggling it in the ear.

"Here, puppies. Follow me."

The dogs gathered around Brogan swarm Helen instead, and she inclines her head toward Brogan. She looks shaken and a little ashamed being caught flirting with a murderer.

"I've got them for now," she assures us. "Call someone to help when you can. Just catch Tom first."

Brogan nods sharply and takes off again, sprinting for the back door of the clinic. Beyond this building are three or four more buildings, all with the same faux rustic decor. He could be hiding in any of them, or he could be hiding in the stables out back. It's impossible to tell. It's likely that we've already lost him, or that we're going to lose him as we sweep the other buildings.

By the time I reach the back door, Brogan is hoisting himself over the low chain-link fence like an acrobat. He lands on his feet, as agile as a cat, and takes off running again.

"Show off," I huff, shuffling after him as fast as my legs will take me. My calves are already burning with the strain, and I'm not even half as fast as Brogan. I need to take Pilates or yoga with Mary sometime, so I'm not laid up for days after cases like this. God willing, there *aren't* more cases like this.

I reach the fence a minute later and fumble with the latch for the gate, opening it after a few seconds of concentrated effort. Brogan darts into one of the outbuildings. On a hunch, I veer off in the opposite direction, toward the stables near the edge of the fence. There isn't much call for them here, because only a few people in the country surrounding Tinsel Pine actually own horses. It's really just myself and Henry Reeves, an ex-vet who used to work here and now runs an informal animal sanctuary on his farmland.

There are few to no animals in the stable to alert us to

Tom's position. He just has to wait until we stop searching, then skip town.

The long square building is dark and foreboding as I approach. There is a shuffle of hooves and a whinny from inside. *So there is a horse or two in here. Probably Henry Reeves's.* I poke my head around the corner, but the setting sun only allows me a short window of light near the door, and whatever is in the gloom beyond is a mystery to me.

There's more shuffling from inside, and then the distinctive sound of a latch being undone. Tom Craft is in the stables. I allow myself a brief mental pat on the back for following my intuition. The indulgent moment is cut short by another distinctive sound. The *clop-clop* of hoofbeats.

I have only seconds to throw to the side of the doorway before a chestnut mare comes flying out at a full gallop. I stare open-mouthed after Tom Craft, who's riding her bareback. Whatever was wrong with the mare seems to be fixed, because she's moving well. I just can't believe that Tom is trying to make his getaway on a *horse*. There's no way for me to catch up to him now. Unless...

I grope for a light switch near the doorway and find it, flicking it on. I blink the spots from my eyes as quickly as I can and scan the room. I find what I'm looking for in the last stall in the back. It's a Dutch Draft with stocky shoulders, feathered legs, a light gray coat, and a similarly colored mane. I almost smile at the thing. It's shorter than the average horse, and so, ideal for my purposes.

When I approach, I do so slowly, even though time is of the essence. I refuse to be as callous as Tom, who probably snatched the horse right out of its stable and spooked the poor girl. The draft horse sniffs my extended palm and snorts once, allowing me to sidle closer to pat the soft side of her neck.

"I need your help, girl," I murmur to her. "We need to catch that bad man. Want to help me?"

She nickers and dips her head. If I were a superstitious woman, I'd say she understands me.

It's difficult, but I eventually manage to heave myself onto her back and nudge her sides with the tips of my snow boots. She starts off at a gentle trot, but works up to speed as we go.

Tom Craft is a receding dot on the horizon. I pass Brogan as he's coming out of the second outbuilding. His jaw drops open and swings in the breeze.

"What are you doing?" he splutters, voice already fading into the distance. "Why are you on a horse?"

"Tom took the other mare. He's heading for the exit. Get to your cruiser and follow us," I call over my shoulder.

I don't get a chance to see if he follows my instructions or not because we're bypassing the low fence, leaping over it as if it's not even there. The Dutch Draft lands nimbly on all fours and makes a self-satisfied sound. I almost chuckle.

"Yes, that *was* good."

Tom's struggling to keep control of his horse just ahead of me. It's clear that he doesn't work with them much, or he'd be able to read the horse's cues. She does *not* want him riding her, and if he continues to shout and kick at her sides, she's going to buck him off. He urges her still faster when he cranes his neck to see who's following behind him.

In the distance, Brogan's siren whirs to life, the siren wailing into the night. It spurs my urgency, and I nudge the draft horse to go faster, trying to close that distance. He's heading toward Oak Creek, which is the last thing we want. These horses aren't trained to work in a city, even one as sleepy as Oak Creek. Holly and Mistletoe were racehorses at one time, used to the hustle and bustle of people and the loud noises that often accompany them.

The poor mare Tom is on will be frightened out of her wits.

The sound of sirens disappears, and I wonder where in tarnation my companion has gotten off to. I really need his help at this point. Tom's about to take a corner hard and fast when suddenly, the siren wails into the night again, accompanied by red and blue lights. This time, it's just ahead of us. Brogan turns his car horizontal before throwing it into park so fast that the wheels kick up a cloud of dust. There's nowhere for Tom to go. The car is too bulky and tall for the horse to make a successful jump over it.

The sirens are the last straw for Tom's mount, and he's unceremoniously bucked off when she rears, hooves flailing, and a horsey scream tearing its way from her throat. Tom goes tumbling tail over teakettle and comes to rest at the base of a pine, knocking into the trunk so hard, he shakes brittle pine needles loose. The sharp, resinous rain only adds insult to injury. His eyes are unfocused, mouth hanging slack. I'm worried he may have a concussion.

Brogan doesn't bother with such trivialities, though. He's out of his car in seconds, pelting over to Tom's side. He's kneeling beside the man, pinning his legs beneath a knee. I don't think it's really necessary at this point. His eyes must be swimming with stars if he's even conscious.

The mare bolts back the way she's come, seeking the familiarity of the Four Legacy Stables. I can't say I blame her.

"I've got him," Brogan says, slipping Tom's hand into a cuff. It closes with the rasp as the metal teeth click into place. "I can't have a horse loose in Glovin County. I'm already pushing my luck by apprehending Tom here, and I have the brass's okay. Could you wrangle her before we have a traffic incident or something equally unfortunate?"

I nod and snap him a salute. "Yes, sir."

He smiles. "That's my girl."

Heat creeps into my cheeks, and I hide a smile of my own. *Okay, so perhaps it hasn't been the worst night after all.*

I mount the Dutch Draft, who has stayed docile and in the same spot, for the most part, picking at the few sprigs of grass that peek up from the snow. I spin around the way we've come, and we begin a trot back to the clinic.

Brogan has this handled. He'll do his job, and I'll focus on mine.

Right now, I have a horse to catch.

CHAPTER SIXTEEN

Tom Craft is held overnight at the Glovin County Jail before being remanded into Brogan's care.

I'm intensely grateful for the delay. Between the impromptu horse ride and all the running I've been up to lately, I'm aching everywhere. I hogged all the water in our home, filling the clawfoot tub to the brim so I could take a steaming Epsom salt bath, leaving my poor daughter to have a lukewarm shower when she returned home from work.

I don't quite understand the odd looks I'm getting when I stroll down the street toward the Tinsel Pine Precinct. I'm only a little bow-legged, and I've combed the graying rat's nest on top of my hair into submission. The high school girls waiting on a bench for their bus push their heads together, hands shielding their mouths so I won't see them snigger. I still hear it, though, and my heart begins to pound, with an unwilling blush creeping into my cheeks. I'm being laughed at, and I don't understand why.

I walk faster, ignoring the ache of my strained muscles. I want to be inside, away from prying eyes. But when I step inside the precinct and knock the slush from my boots, it's no better.

Officer Terry is sitting at the front desk, cradling a cup of coffee. The Golden Caff's signature logo—a steaming golden cup—is printed onto the side of the cardboard sleeve. He nurses the beverage like it's liquid life, clearly not used to being up so early. I'm not sure why he's here since he's normally on the night shift.

He's a little younger than Brogan, but no less gruff. He's got a round face, a weak chin, and blue-green eyes that always look a little watery. He's neither thin nor fat, and his clothes always toe the line between disheveled and outright slovenly. The impression is made even worse this morning by the residue of powdered donuts on his sleeve and the trail of coffee that's dribbled down his collar.

He raises his eyes, and benign disinterest flickers to a searing glare.

"What are you doing here?" he demands.

I balk in the doorway. Officer Terry has always been terse with me, skirting around outright telling me that he doesn't like me dating his boss. He's never been so blatantly rude, though.

"I'm here to see how the investigation is going. Brogan asked me to stop in."

"That's Chief Peterson to you, civilian," he says hotly. "And you're just a consultant. You don't have a place in that interrogation room. Especially not after the stunt you pulled."

"Stunt?" I echo, bewildered. What's he talking about? I haven't done anything reckless or stupid recently. Is he referring to my encounter with Rose Fletcher? That happened days ago. Surely he's had time to cool off about that.

He lifts the *Tinsel Pine Herald* from his desk and shakes it menacingly in my direction. I'm expecting him to roll it into a tube and whack me for being a bad dog.

Instead, he hurls it at me, and I barely get my arm up in time to keep it from hitting me right in the noggin. I scrabble to catch it, and when I do, the front page is wrinkled. Not so wrinkled that the headline isn't legible, however.

Local Hero Hunts Criminal on Horseback.

A million little grayscale dots form a picture beneath the words. It's grainy, dark, and a little blurry, but my heart sinks all the same. Because there's no mistaking who's sitting astride the Dutch Draft. I'm hunched forward, pressing into the back of my steed. It's not a flattering picture. My hair is all over the place, my shirt riding up, and the expression on my face is darn near comical.

Someone—a certain vet tech leaps to mind—photographed the chase and passed this on to the local reporter Brad Witt. Aside from the murder that happened last month, not much goes on in Tinsel Pine. It's all celebrations, tourism, and human-interest stories. He probably lapped this up like a cat with cream.

"You're making us look like a laughingstock!" Officer Terry explodes. "So just turn around and walk out the door, Green. You're not needed here."

A voice snaps like a whip from the hall and startles us both. I turn almost at the same time as Officer Terry to see Brogan in the doorway, face a rictus of anger, pale eyes fixed on Officer Terry.

"Sit down and mind your tongue, officer. You're not in charge here. Carol was invited to join me."

"Sir," Officer Terry begins in a more respectful tone. "With all due respect, you have to consider how this looks. She rents out a sleigh for rides. She's got no experience, and furthermore, you're dating her. It's going to cause talk."

Brogan shrugs. "Let them talk. Carol has turned up more leads in a few weeks than the rest of us combined. Like it or not, we need her assistance. If you have a problem with it, you can go, Officer Terry. I'll make Dawson work a double shift if I have to. The young man could use the overtime pay."

Officer Terry's shoulders slump, and he settles back into his seat with the air of a petulant teenager. "That won't be necessary, sir. I've got this covered."

"Good," Brogan grunts. "Come on, Carol."

He turns on his heel without another word and gestures for me to follow him. I scamper down the hall after him, more grateful for his defense than words could ever express. I'll try to articulate it tonight with dinner.

Unlike the last time a suspect was in custody, I enter the room this time. Tom Craft's face is pinched, and he massages his temples with the hand that isn't handcuffed to a chair. I bet he has a goose egg the size of a bowling ball after the tumble he took. Brogan doesn't look at all sympathetic as he draws out a chair for me to sit in, and then drops his bulk into the one beside it.

"Got any aspirin?" Tom asks. "They say caffeine's supposed to help with a headache, but..." He gestures vaguely at the Styrofoam cup half-full of burnt coffee that sits on the table in front of him. "This is doing diddly for me."

"Fresh out," Brogan says, tone vaguely suggesting he might be enjoying the other man's pain. "Give me a confession, and I might be able to procure some."

Tom Craft finally cracks those smoldering brown eyes open and fixes us both with a glare. "That's extortion, you know. Even criminals have rights."

"Maybe, but I don't owe you jack, Tom. I know you killed those two women. We tested the Borax can in your house and found traces of strychnine in the powder. You used it to try to kill your mistress. And you stole Tramadol from your work to poison your soon-to-be ex-wife."

Tom sits up straighter. "I never did that."

"Which time do you mean, Tom? The time you poisoned your wife or the time you poisoned your girlfriend? You can give either confession first. The order doesn't really matter to me."

"I didn't kill Skye," he grits out. "I admit, I tried to get rid of Rose. She knew too much. If she'd guessed, she would have..."

He trails off, pressing that compellingly full mouth into a thin line until his lips turn white with the strain of holding in the words.

"Knew too much about what, Tom?" Brogan asks.

"Nothing. She knew nothing. I just wanted her gone," he mutters. "Always pressuring me for a ring. Who wouldn't want to be rid of a harpy like that?"

"Is that why you killed Skye?" I ask. "Was she a harpy, too?"

He snorts. "A harpy and a half. But I didn't poison her."

"Forgive me if I'm skeptical," Brogan says. "You have admitted to attempted murder. It's just a hop, skip, and a jump to homicide, Tom."

Tom shoves a hand into his hair and sets his mouth into that hard line again, trying to rein in his anger.

"Look, I thought about it, okay? I wanted her dead almost every day since the divorce. She could never make things easy. She just wanted to take and take and take until I had nothing left. But I never went through with it. And I wouldn't have had to kill Rose if she didn't know."

Again, he seems to feel as though he's said too much because he closes his mouth and crosses his arms tightly around his chest. Before Brogan can come up with a line of questioning, Tom speaks again.

"Wouldn't you want to, Chief? I know you have your own woman troubles. Isn't Sharona trying to take Columbo? All women are shrews, trying to steal from good, hard-working men."

Brogan's eyes narrow. "I've wanted to blister Sharona's backside a few times, but no, I've never wanted to kill her. Normal, sane people don't try to off their exes, Tom. Confess to Skye's murder, and maybe the DA can cut you a deal. Maybe your sentence will be life in prison instead of the death penalty."

Tom shrugs his shoulders. "Yeah, sure. Why not? You're going to keep digging until you find something that you can finger me with. So sure, I killed my ex-wife. She pushed me too far, tried to take my kids, yadda, yadda, so forth. Fill in the rest. I don't really care."

This seems good enough for Brogan, who writes down the confession. But I'm leery. Maybe it's an act, and he's pretending to be a (somewhat) innocent man. Maybe he's playing me for a sucker.

But for whatever reason, I actually believe him. Being guilty of the attempted murder doesn't necessarily equate to being guilty of the successful homicide. There's another killer out there. I can feel it.

Now, to convince Brogan of the same.

CHAPTER SEVENTEEN

"Thank you for clearing my name, Miss Green," Azalea says for the umpteenth time. "And thank you for this job. It means a lot."

I smile again, but it's hard to maintain my earlier enthusiasm. It's not totally Azalea's fault that I'm moody. I'm still convinced that Tom Craft isn't solely responsible for his wife's death. Brogan vehemently disagrees and, since he's the lead investigator on the case, I've been outvoted. The case is closed. Tom is going away for a long time.

That nags at me. What if he's going away for a crime he's not responsible for? He's a repugnant man with Adonis good looks and little else in his favor. He's proved himself capable of attempting murder by trying to axe off his girlfriend. So why is it so hard to swallow that he could have killed Skye as well?

"No problem, Azalea. Are you ready to meet them?"

Azalea's sweet smile smooths the ragged edges of my nerves, bringing the circular quest for answers to a halt for a second. I can't believe we ever thought this girl could be capable of murder.

"Yes. I hear that Clark is excited to see me. I used to babysit for Skye all the time before all those accusations were slung around. She probably thought I'd sell off her family heirlooms or something. She didn't pay me well, and she was always snotty, but I really liked the kids. I'm happy their grandparents are letting us take this sleigh ride with them."

So am I. I need to see that no lasting damage has been done to their poor little psyches by an unhinged Tom Craft.

The sleigh slides to a stop before a little cottage-style house with a postage-stamp yard. There's a tricycle by the front steps that's half-buried in snow. The little ones are waiting on the steps, bundled in puffy blue and green coats, their hoods cinched tight, gloves and scarves on, and snow boots that nearly reach their knees.

Both Clark and his sister look better. They stand straighter and look us straight in the eye as they approach. Their dazzling little grins melt my heart. I love children. I'd like a grandbaby of my own to spoil, but Mary insists she'll chuck the copy of *What to Expect When You're Expecting* I bought her at my head as a hint if I ask her again for an ETA.

They clamber into the sleigh, greeting us both in chirpy little voices. Yes, it's definitely a good thing Tom Craft is gone. I can't imagine what sort of future these little angels had to look forward to with him as a father.

Edward and Lillian Adams lean over the side of the sleigh to plant kisses on their heads before standing back to wave. They've aged well. I can't tell either are in their seventies. Lillian still has a hint of ashy brown peeking through the gray. Edward's salt and pepper hair has barely receded, and paired with his horn-rimmed glasses and sweater vest, he looks like an aging scholar.

"Thank you, Miss Green," Serena says in a small voice from the back of the sleigh.

I crane my neck to look at her. She's got her hands folded

114

primly in her lap, and the folds of a tulle ballerina skirt peek out from beneath the edge of her heavy down coat. The tip of her cute upturned nose is already turning red from cold, but she doesn't seem to mind. She's offering me a small smile, trying her best to overcome her natural shyness.

"What for?"

"Daddy was a bad man. He hurt mommy. So you and the chief put him away. Thank you for that."

The warmth of her praise is tempered by a sense of disgust aimed directly at their father. These kids shouldn't be familiar with horror, pain, murder, or monsters. What a horrid situation, to know at six years old that your father deliberately hurt your mother. Even my poor Mary hasn't suffered so.

"Of course, Serena. Do you like living with your grandparents?"

That little grin grows wider, showing perfect milky teeth. "Yeah. Grandma is nice, and we bake cookies and stuff together. She's going to teach me how to make peppermint pigs when I'm older, like the ones mommy made."

"That's great!" I say, pumping as much enthusiasm as I can muster into my voice, swallowing back the sense of revulsion that still lingers. I don't know why I'm convinced that Tom isn't guilty. He's proven himself capable of a whole host of nastiness. Why not attribute this to him as well?

Because one thing doesn't equate to another, not even in a murder investigation. A search of the Four Legacy Clinic has turned up no inconsistencies. With a staff of fifteen, someone would have noticed that amount of medication going missing, surely? The entire clinic isn't in on the conspiracy to kill Skye—of that I'm certain. Helen helped us and continues to be forthright when we come to her with questions, so I don't think Tom has an inside man or woman covering his behind, either.

"Are you okay, Miss Green?" Azalea asks, thankfully keeping her voice low, so the inquisitive ears behind us don't pick up on what she's saying. "You look a little pale."

"I'm fine," I say, my voice coming out a half-sigh of exasperation. "I'm just thinking. And there's no need for formality, Lea. You can call me Carol."

"Were you thinking about something scary? You don't look so good."

That is probably the long bouts of insomnia plaguing me. I'm driving Mary absolutely crazy, getting up at all hours of the night to pace the floor like a restless ghost. She's threatening to move into Marcy's house until I settle down. She's planning a party this weekend for my benefit, thinking that a distraction will do me good. It's black tie and something that her grandmother would probably like. Instead of calming me down, it's just given me another unpleasant thing to occupy my thoughts.

"Not scary, per se. Worrying."

Azalea tilts her head like a curious bird. "About me? If you don't want me to work here—"

"Not you, Lea," I say, reaching over to pat her knee in what I hope will be a comforting gesture. I dart a glance toward the back where the children are chattering happily to each other. Serena occasionally sticks out her tongue to catch a falling snowflake. "I'm worried about the investigation. About Tom."

"What's there to worry about? He's been put away, hasn't he? He's gone, and everyone's better off."

"That's just it," I say, lowering my voice even further. This is not a discussion that I should be having in front of the children. "I'm not sure that Tom did it."

Azalea leans in close so she can hear me and respond in kind. "But he was arrested for trying to kill his girlfriend.

116

They weren't even married. He had a lot to lose if Skye won the custody battle."

She glances back at the children as well. "I know my mom and dad were pretty mad at each other and were going to split when I was little. It didn't happen, but a lot of my friends' parents are divorced. It's never pretty. I think he probably killed her."

"Maybe," I admit. "But the lack of proof is bothering me. For Rose Fletcher's attempt, we found the spiked Borax. But for this? Nothing. No Tramadol missing from the clinic, no prescription for it in his home. Nothing. There's no evidence he had it. No record of buying the wine, either."

"Rose Fletcher bought wine," Azalea says, rubbing a hand over her cheek thoughtfully. "I remember when the rumors circulated the town. Everyone was saying that you guys were accusing her of poisoning the wine when she had her choking fit. Could it have been a team effort?"

"That's what I thought," I say with another sigh. "But the search of her home only found the wine and no pills. Brogan looked into it thoroughly. She's got no health problems except for a ragweed allergy that flares up in spring. The strongest thing in her medicine cabinet was codeine cough syrup."

"And that wasn't what was used to kill her." Azalea shakes her head. "I don't know, Miss G. I still think he did it."

"He probably did, but I want to be sure. I have to find more clues."

Azalea's lips tug into a smile. "I'll tell you what. This weekend, I'll swing by your house with some of the things I stole from Skye. It's some paperwork, receipts, the pig, and makeup I stole from her purse. Maybe something in there can help."

I raise an imperious brow. "I thought you *just* stole the

pig. Isn't that what you said the other day?"

Azalea scuffs her shoes sheepishly on the floor of the sled. "Okay, I lied a little bit. I thought it would sound better if I didn't admit to the other stuff."

"You have to be honest with me, Lea, or this partnership won't work. Is that all you took? Be honest."

She placed a hand over her heart and held the other up solemnly. "Give me a stack of bibles, and I'll swear on them."

I relaxed back into my seat. That was good enough for me. Perhaps it wasn't such a bad thing that Azalea was a sticky-fingered reprobate. Maybe the proof that would lay my mind to rest would be in what she'd thieved from Skye's things.

"Alright. This weekend isn't great for me, though. I'm supposed to be attending my daughter's party," I say. It came out as if I'd said, "I'm being dragged to watch a puppy evisceration."

Azalea chuckles at the look on my face. "It's not a big deal, Miss G. My mom and I got an invitation, too, seeing as you're my boss now and all. It was really nice of her. I'll bring the stuff in a bag, shall I?"

"Yes, I suppose that's fine."

At least one good thing will come of the party now. I can lay my suspicions to rest at last. Prove once and for all that Tom is the scuzzbag everyone believes him to be.

The rest of the ride passes in relative silence, except for the giggling of the children in the backseat. I give the Adamses more than their money's worth, carting the children to every beautiful or fun locale I can think of. By the time we return, they've got a box of donuts wedged between them on the seat, courtesy of Leon Frost, the local baker, and a steaming cup of hot chocolate each, compliments of the Golden Caff. Pretty much everyone seems to be celebrating Tom's arrest.

I watch the pair fondly until they reach the front door of their grandparents' house and disappear inside. This day should be perfect. So why can't I banish thoughts of Tom Craft? He isn't worth leasing mind space to.

Azalea and I attend to a few more appointments before the day is through. We're near her home when we spy a lone figure trudging through the snow, his head down, bracing against the wind. It takes a minute to place him, even though I've seen him two or three times this month. It's a man in his mid-to-late thirties, with a head of thinning black hair and a face that borders on being a little plain. His spectacles catch the light as he walks.

We pull alongside him, and I call out a greeting.

"Hey there, Mr. King!"

He jerks in surprise and yanks his gaze from his own feet to look at us. They flicker from me to Azalea, his eyes narrowing in dislike when he sees her.

"Hello, Miss Green." Then he grudgingly adds, "Miss Marshall."

"Vaughn," Azalea says curtly, lobbing the name like an insult. King's shoulders stiffen with dislike, and I'm about three seconds from flinging my body between them to prevent the catfight I feel coming.

"What are you doing here?" Vaughn asks me, letting his eyes slide past Azalea as if she's not even there. His casual dismissal of her personhood bothers me, but I suppose there's some weight to that old adage, "If you can't say something nice..."

"Finishing up my workday. How about you? Ready for the party this weekend?"

Vaughn fishes a handkerchief from his inside pocket and dabs at his nose. "I'm afraid not. I'm coming down with something and don't want to pass it on. Do give her my regards, though, will you?"

Oh, if only I could be so fortunate.

"Of course. Do you want a ride home?"

Vaughn's smile is a second late and more than a little weary. "I'm fine, Miss Green."

His face is almost the same white as the surrounding snow. All but his nose, which flames red from cold and chafing. His eyes water, and he looks thoroughly miserable.

"Have you seen a doctor? I could take you to the clinic the next town over if you'd prefer."

Vaughn waves the suggestion away. "I said I'm fine. I'll down a gallon of orange juice, gorge myself on chicken soup, and have an extended staycation at home. I hear channel nineteen will be marathoning *Quincy, M.E.* all this week. Maybe I'll watch that. Pretend I'm half the sleuth you and Brogan are while I try to guess the culprit."

I shrug. "If you're sure."

"Quite sure. Good night, Miss Green."

He ignores Azalea entirely and trudges stubbornly through the drifts that block the sidewalk. Azalea glares at him until he rounds the corner a block later.

"Jerk," she mumbles. "He deserves that cold."

"Don't be rude," I chide her as we set off again. "He's had enough hardship as it is, after losing his friend and business partner. I'm sure things have just been a little jumbled, and that's why he made the most recent accusation."

Azalea just purses her lips and stares frostily ahead until the route is done, and I drop her home.

Perhaps it's good they won't be attending the party together, I reason. Azalea looks ready to stab someone with a fork. It'd be a shame to have another murder on our hands after solving the most recent one, wouldn't it? I just hope whatever she brings will provide the answers I'm looking for.

CHAPTER EIGHTEEN

"I don't see why you insist on making this difficult."

Brogan adjusts his tie for the tenth time, tugging at it uncomfortably as though it's a noose about to strangle him. He looks a little miserable in a black suit and starched white shirt. Black-tie formal is definitely not Brogan's style. Although I love how the cut of the suit frames his body, I won't ask something like this of him again. This party is Mary's idea anyway, not mine. She press-ganged us both into attending. I'm pretty sure that Brogan hasn't worn this suit since he married and isn't planning to wear it again until he waits at the altar one last time.

I'm wearing my only black dress at Mary's insistence. Even with the Spanx to hold my fluffy tummy in check, I think it's a little too form-fitting. Brogan seems to like it, though. When he isn't putting out the aura of a man on the brink of hulking out of his suit, he's admiring my legs.

"I'm not being difficult," I insist, straightening his tie patiently. "I just think that there's something off about this whole thing. It's all a little too easy, don't you think?"

It's been almost a week since Tom Craft was charged

with murder and attempted murder. He's been sent to county jail pending trial. Unbelievably, Rose Fletcher has been to visit him. Not to curse him out, as I might have done in her position, but to propose marriage so they could have conjugal visits. I shake my head softly. I will never understand some women.

"It's cut and dry for a reason, Carol," he says impatiently, tugging at the tie again so it's laying crookedly. I don't try to straighten it again, reasoning it's a lost cause at this point. "Tom Craft was a misogynistic piece of work who tried to kill his girlfriend and succeeded in killing his wife. We're lucky he didn't move onto his kids next. He doesn't seem to like them very much, does he?"

I shudder. I *am* grateful that Tom Craft has been put away before he can do more damage to his children. What I've witnessed already is horrific enough, and I can't imagine what their future might have been like if he'd remained their sole guardian. They're much better off with Skye's parents, Edward and Lillian, than they'll ever be with their father. Edward and Lillian are both aging, but Azalea has offered to babysit for the kids on the days she isn't working for me. It's earned her a ticket to tonight's soiree—though she won't be drinking the white wine, of course.

"Maybe, but I just have a gut feeling, Brogan. I know I don't have evidence and that feelings aren't admissible in court. I just don't think he killed Skye. Call me crazy."

"You're bonkers, Carol," he says with a gently amused smile. He presses his lips to my forehead to take the sting out of the insult. It makes me smile, just a little. He murmurs against my hair and gives me a gentle squeeze. "Can you just turn your brain off for an hour? It's a party, after all. I promise I'll stay sober so we can duck out after the appetizers are served. We can order a pizza here, and I promise you can wear your sweatpants and ratty nightshirt while we watch reruns of *Law and Order*."

I wrap my arms around his neck and plant a wet kiss on his lips. I'll have to reapply the coral lipstick in the car, but I don't care.

"You're going to make me fall in love with you, Brogan Peterson," I say in a faux scolding tone.

His answering grin is unrepentant, even as he wipes the imprint of my lipstick off his mouth. "That's the plan."

He places a gentle, guiding hand at the small of my back and escorts me out of his living room. It's spitting snow again, though I doubt this stuff will stick. He keeps me close, half-shielding me from the wind until we reach his car. The real one, this time, not the police cruiser. He surprises me by driving a fuel-efficient Jetta instead of one of the boxy Hummers or SUVs that all men of a certain age seem to gravitate toward. It's a far cry from Tom Craft's bright red Dodge Viper, or the "mid-life crisis mobile," as it's been affectionately dubbed.

I suppose Brogan isn't as insecure as I originally guessed.

It's a fifteen-minute drive to the Ivy Pavilion. The place is classically elegant and a popular venue for weddings. Mary is living up to her grandmother's training, hosting the party at the ritziest place in town. The place is a New Colonial Manor house set on about six acres of land, all of it bursting with colorful flowers, with careful paths cut to the house, the gazebo, and marble dance floor in the back. Or so I'm told. Right now, it's all coated in snow, glistening white and silver in the reflection of a million twinkling lights. Soft classical music drifts from the partially open door.

This party is being funded by Irene, who believes the best pick-me-up after a crisis is a get-together where people who don't particularly like each other are forced to make polite small talk for hours on end. The whole thing reeks of money and pretentiousness, and it's yet another reason I want to be a million miles away from it.

I'm guessing Mary has kept the finer points to herself. If Irene knows the party celebrates the end of a murder investigation that I helped suss out, she'll be having heart palpitations. I won't rob Mary of her joy, though, no matter how much I hate the idea of this party. Skye Adams was her friend, and she's been taking it hard. As far as she and everyone else is concerned, her murderer is behind bars, and justice has been served. Maybe I should just get with the times and put this whole thing behind me as well.

"One hour," Brogan promises me before we exit our respective seats. "Then we get pizza, and I get out of this monkey suit."

"Sounds like a plan," I say, hoisting a smile onto my lips. *Grin and bear it, Carol. Grin and bear it.*

We're greeted by a doorman, of all things, who takes our coats and hangs them neatly on a rack beside the door before giving us each a ticket saying he's done so. I shake my head. I will never, ever be comfortable at events like these.

Thankfully, the guest list is small: Brogan and me, Officers Dawson and Terry, Azalea and her mother, Marcy Gourd, and a few other friends. Vaughn King was on the guest list as well, but decided to bow out after contracting a cold. Irene will be preparing him a little plate with the hors d'oeuvres, a helping of the entrée, and a thermos with wine, dropping it by his house before the night is over.

Neither officer looks comfortable in their suits, either, though Dawson looks almost as dapper as Brogan in his. Officer Terry won't look at either of us, still smarting from the chastisement he's gotten from Brogan. Good manners. If you don't have anything nice to say...

Azalea looks pleased, though, sporting a new violet dress with ruffled sleeves and a flared skirt, her blond hair arranged into an elegant French braid. I've already alerted Mary to be on the lookout for missing flatware or china. Azalea will have a hard time smuggling anything but a soup spoon in her tiny sequined clutch, which makes me feel better. She sips at punch while Nora finishes a glass of white wine and waves over a waiter to provide another. I suppose that means Azalea is the designated driver tonight. Maybe I'll sneak them both out early and escort them home in my sleigh.

There's a four-legged guest in attendance as well, one I'm not expecting. Bruno waits in a corner, tail casually thumping every time a guest comes near him. Someone's put him in a bowtie, which almost disappears beneath his jowls every time he opens his doggy mouth to smile or yawn. It's adorable, in a way, but I'm not entirely sure why he's here. Occasionally, I see Azalea wander close to him and discreetly drop one of the salmon at his feet. The dog chuffs in thanks before devouring the whole thing whole, and then licking her hand.

Mary is mingling near the punchbowl. She's deep in conversation with Dawson, who's leaning forward, elbow propped on one eggshell-white wall. He's got a soft, pleased smile on his full mouth, and that look that men sometimes get—and women overlook. The subtle art of affection is often lost on the fairer sex when men apply it for the first time.

I stare at them long enough that Brogan prompts me to move forward, tugging me out of the entryway and into the hall proper.

Perhaps I should be feeling defensive or happy, or even a little stunned at this new development. But instead, I only feel a sense of benign interest. I've really only known Dawson for a month and change. And, sad as it is to say, I've only known Mary for a few years longer. The time apart means I still have so much more to learn about her likes and dislikes, including her taste in men. It's almost like watching two strangers flirt. I'm not sure how I should feel at this moment, watching Dawson put the moves on my daughter.

When I approach the pair, Dawson leans away, shoving his hands sheepishly in his pockets, like a schoolboy caught in the act of wrongdoing. Mary's face breaks into a wide grin, her eyes sweeping over me.

"I'm so glad you made it! And you look fantastic, Mom. You should wear evening wear more often."

I screw a smile in place rather than respond that I'll take a root canal without anesthesia over this any day.

"This party is nice. But why is Bruno here? Shouldn't he be with Rose Fletcher by now? She's been released from the hospital, right? Or was I imagining that?"

Mary purses her lips, displeasure stealing across her face.

"Rose Fletcher is moving to Glovin County to be closer to Tom. She's convinced she's getting that ring from him, and given what he has to look forward to, he'll probably say yes. None of the apartment complexes in Oak Creek will allow her to keep a dog, so he's currently homeless. I'm trying to find him a nice owner. I really think it'd be a shame to send him out to Henry Reeves's animal shelter. Dogs need one-on-one attention. But it's a little difficult to find someone who wants a dog essentially trained as a pickpocket."

"That would be difficult. Maybe you should advertise his skill as a selling feature? Like for children's parties?"

"Maybe."

Azalea sidles up to us, pausing at my elbow, tugging discreetly on my sleeve. When I turn to look at her, she's clutching something hard to her side. It looks like a blue and green backpack patterned with a celebrity's face. She's careful not to let Brogan see it. My heart pounds. Finally, I might be able to put this nagging sense of doubt to rest once and for all.

"Hold that thought for just a second, Mary. I need to sneak off to the little girl's room."

"Me, too," Azalea pipes up, linking her arm with mine. "We can go together."

Dawson chuckles as if I've just told a joke. I slip away from our little band before the stale jokes can start. I want to like Dawson, but hearing a few sexist one-liners meant to impress Mary won't warm me to him.

Azalea winds through the maze of tables and chairs that dot the room, pulling me to a stop when we finally reach an alcove tucked in near the back. Bruno follows us, hopefully sniffing at Azalea's hand for more illicit treats.

"Is it all in there?" I ask eagerly, rubbing my hands together nervously. They're trembling slightly, in a way they haven't been since Rose Fletcher came after me with a bat.

"Yep. Everything I managed to snatch. It's not much, and I don't think it's anything damning, but you're welcome to look."

She unzips the top and pulls it open wide so I can peer at the contents. There's a sheaf of paper, a few crumpled receipts, a tube of lipstick, and the peppermint pig. I'm a little disappointed, if I'm honest. She's right that there's not much here.

"This is all you managed to steal?"

Azalea nods and opens her mouth to respond, but never gets the chance to speak before Bruno rises to his feet and lunges forward. At the word "steal", he snatches the bag in his heavy jaws and takes off like a shot, knocking aside a few chairs and Officer Terry. The latter staggers back into one of the tables, knocking the rosewater and tea-light centerpiece to the floor. The glass shatters upon impact, and Officer

Terry makes a pratfall worthy of a *Tom and Jerry* cartoon, spilling punch all over his pristine dress shirt.

He's still swearing as I race after the dog, narrowly avoiding my own accident. He's clearing a path through the guests and making a beeline for the door. I chase after him as fast as I can, but as proven before, I'm no match for the dog.

That would have been it for my short-lived plan if Brogan hadn't intervened. He lunges forward, catching the dog around the neck, and takes them both to the floor in a tangle of limbs. Somehow Bruno gets the backpack straps caught on his four doggy paws and can't climb to his feet again.

My heart sinks when I see the contents of the bag splayed out on the floor.

Brogan snatches the papers and the pigs before I can clean up the mess, and I'm left to untangle the poor dog from his restraints. He climbs to his feet with a whine and nudges the backpack away with his nose.

"Bad dog," I scold. I know I shouldn't be angry with him. It's Tom Craft's machinations that led the poor pooch to purloin things in the first place. But I've been outed to Brogan, and there's an inches-long rip in the thigh of my pantyhose from the effort it took to run after him. It's safe to say I'm not in a charitable mood.

Brogan's eyes flick up to me, and they've gone hard and steely. I take a step back from him, chin dropping to my chest as his accusation spears me. Trust. I demand it from him, but I haven't followed through on my end. Shame rises in a flush along my neck and into my ears.

"Brogan, I—"

"Don't," he says flatly. "Don't start, Carol. I told you to drop it."

Nora, Dawson, Azalea, and Terry crowd around us while the servers do their darndest to pretend nothing out of the ordinary is happening. I have to admire their professionalism after the debacle that's just played out before them.

"Drop what?" Mary asks.

"Carol has this suspicion that Tom Craft is innocent of Skye's murder when it's clear that he had the resources and the motivation to pull it off."

"The records don't show that any Tramadol went missing—"

"He could have stolen it before they stocked a thing, Carol," Brogan says hotly. "Or he could have bought it off someone with cash, so there'd be no paper trail. It's him."

Mary steps between us, hands outstretched, pressing her palms flat against each of our chests.

"This is a party," she insists, glaring at both of us in turn. "No fighting. We can talk about it later."

"Fine," Brogan huffs. "We'll talk tomorrow. Suddenly, I'm not really in the mood for that pizza and a nightcap we were discussing."

My hands ball into fists at my sides. Stubborn, impossible man. Revoking our plans for the evening is just petty.

Azalea snatches the pig up from the ground and holds it out to us, a note of desperate anxiety coloring her tone as she says, "This thing is supposed to be good luck if you break it, right? Why don't we all take a piece home with us?"

Brogan's shoulders are still stiff with displeasure as he takes the pig from Azalea. He marches over to the table, and then raps the pig on the side of it like he's cracking an egg. It takes a few tries before a fissure begins to appear in the pig's side. Brogan places the pig on the table and pries it the rest of the way open with a grunt. It comes apart with a crack.

And a shower of tiny glittering gems come spilling out onto the silvery tablecloth.

"Are those...?" Mary asks in a hushed whisper.

"Diamonds," Dawson says, plucking one up from the table so he can examine it. He turns it over several times in his palm before holding it up to the light. "I'm no jeweler. Are these real?"

Mary takes one as well, and her eyes grow round as she examines it. "They are."

I trust her judgment on the matter. She grew up around wealth and with a grandmother who just adored shopping for new jewelry. If any casual observer will know their stuff, it'll be Mary.

Brogan's eyes swivel to Azalea, a scowl carving furrows into his already stony face. "Explain this."

She backs away, hands flying up in surrender. Tears actually shine in her eyes.

"I didn't know that was in there. I swear. Or I would never..."

The gears in my brain whirr to life, moving smoothly after so many days of grinding in futility. The pieces slot into place with a satisfying click, and the picture becomes clear.

"It's not Azalea, Brogan. Please stop shouting at her."

"Oh? Because from where I'm standing, this looks like an excellent motive for murder. This is the missing merchandise Skye and Vaughn have been reporting."

Brogan is already reaching for his handcuffs. He stuffs them inside his coat pocket, just in case, along with a taser. Some habits you just can't break, like coming prepared for every situation. I stop him, gently locking a hand around his wrist before he can get a hand on them.

"It *is* an excellent motive for murder, but Azalea didn't do it."

"Then who did it exactly?"

I take a deep breath to tell them what I desperately hope is true and not just the ramblings of a dippy old woman.

"It was Vaughn King. And I know how he did it."

CHAPTER NINETEEN

Mary, Brogan, Dawson, Bruno, and I all squeeze into Brogan's Jetta, moving toward the precinct as we can without the convenience of lights and sirens. It becomes even harder to move around in the backseat when we swap vehicles, piling into the squad car next. Bruno is stuffed in the middle of the back seat, his bulk pushing us to either side. My face is plastered uncomfortably against the glass as we speed through the city.

On a hunch, Brogan flicks the lights and sirens off a few blocks before we reach the strip mall. It's after regular hours, so theoretically, the store should be closed. But when we pull up in front of Skye High Jewelry, a weak light is wavering from somewhere inside.

"Well, I'll be a monkey's uncle. You were right, Carol." He casts me a look in the rearview mirror that is torn somewhere between frustration and wonderment. "I think you went into the wrong line of work, Carol. You'd make a fantastic detective."

The praise brings warmth into my cheeks. I wave it away

and hide my smile. "Flatter me later, Brogan. We need to catch him in the act first."

"Right."

He and Dawson climb out first, and then open the doors for Mary, Bruno, and me to exit. If all goes well, we'll need to walk home and let Dawson and Brogan haul Vaughn off to jail.

"Stay here," Brogan orders.

"Brogan, you can't be serious—"

"I'm deadly serious, Carol. If you're right, he's already killed someone to keep this secret."

"With poison, not brute force. Vaughn King isn't some sort of Terminator, Brogan. He doesn't look like he's done a day of exercise in his life. What could go wrong with you and Dawson present?"

"A million things, Carol. He could have a knife or a gun. He could run or fight. He could hurt you or Mary. I'm not willing to take that chance, even if you are. You're important to me. Don't get yourself killed trying to prove something to yourself or me."

His words diffuse my carefully crafted defense, and I deflate. He's right, of course. It doesn't matter if Vaughn King isn't physically formidable if he's armed. I've been on the business end of a gun once before, and I'm not looking forward to being there again. The person who'd had me there turned out to be innocent, so I hadn't been shot. I won't get that lucky a second time.

"Fine," I mutter. "But let us wait outside the door."

Brogan thinks about it for half a second and then decides that it's the best compromise that we can reach on short notice. "Five hundred feet back and out of sight. Hide underneath the awning of Nelson's shop and wait until we have him in the car to approach."

"Deal."

Together, we sneak forward, staying as light on our toes as possible, taking a circuitous route to avoid the CCTV surveillance on the building. Mary and I obediently halt beneath the awning to James Nelson's shop and wait. Nerves riot furiously in my stomach as Brogan approaches the door of Skye High Jewelry and tests the handle.

The door swings open without a sound. So we were right —he's inside. Brogan withdraws a gun from the shoulder rig he'd hastily strapped on before we left the precinct. He looks like a shorter, stockier James Bond as he creeps forward, gun pointed at the ground. Dawson follows, gun still in his holster.

Mary and Bruno vibrate with nervous energy at my side. Mary chews her knuckle every few seconds.

"I just can't believe this," she whispers. "I knew and liked them both. They got along so well. How could he just...kill her like that? I couldn't kill my friends."

I shrug. "Greed is a very powerful motivator."

"Still. Could you kill Marcy or Azalea over something like money?"

I don't answer. The truth is, I'm not sure. Of course, I like to believe nothing in the world could ever compel me to hurt the ones I love. But the truth is, we never know. Not until that pivotal moment when you're down to the wire and the hard decisions have to be made.

I lean forward, heart throbbing painfully in my chest as I strain to hear what's happening in the shop.

There's a crash and a clatter from inside, and then Vaughn's startled voice wafts from the half-open door.

"C-Chief! I didn't hear you come in. What are you doing here at this hour?"

I can just picture Brogan taking a slow, deliberate step forward, keeping his gun out of sight.

"I could ask you the same question, Vaughn. What are

you doing up so late? I was told you have a cold. Isn't that why you couldn't attend the party tonight?"

"I...erm...got a bit of a second wind and wanted to finish up some things here before this thing takes me down for good. I'm still contagious and didn't want to spread this around, you know."

"Uh-huh," Brogan drawls. "Nausea, dizziness, headache, vomiting, and weakness can all be symptoms of the flu. They can also be the side effects of Tramadol. You had to drink a little of the wine to sell it, didn't you, Vaughn?"

"I don't know what you mean," Vaughn says in a shaky voice. "This is just ludicrous. Skye was my best friend. How dare you even—"

"We know you and she were smuggling diamonds out of this shop with her peppermint pigs, Vaughn. You were selling them. But she slipped one into the regular batch she was giving to the investors that day, right? It spooked her enough to call it quits, and you couldn't have that."

"Preposterous," Vaughn splutters. "Absolutely preposterous."

"And then, one of them went missing when Bruno and Azalea turned up at town hall. It must have been a nightmare for you. Your merchandise missing, and your partner ready to bail. Nora can confirm you visited that day to make another accusation about her daughter. You slipped into her bathroom before she gave you the boot. So you took her husband's prescription, ground it up, and put it in Skye's favorite wine, which you probably had on hand."

There's an eerie silence from Vaughn as Brogan continues to lay out his case. I can picture his Adam's apple bobbing like a cork as he struggles to swallow. Dry mouth can be a symptom of Tramadol overdose as well. I wonder who he's dosed recently to hide his crimes. One of the other employees? We'll have to check on them just as soon as he's in custody. There's no telling who's in danger.

"You brought the wine and something to eat, most likely. Apologized for overreacting, got her on the subject of her ex-husband to keep her drinking while you only had a few swallows of your own drink. Heck, she probably finished that glass, too, when you were gone. And then, she collapsed in her kitchen, solving your problem quite nicely."

Vaughn's voice comes out level and eerily calm. "I knew I should have spiked your punch. That meddling woman doesn't know when to stop, does she? Couldn't just let it rest on Tom Craft's shoulders like everybody else."

Mary has her knuckles shoved into her mouth to contain a sound of horror. I don't say I told you so. I think the poor girl has suffered enough. First, Azalea, Bruno, and I had conspired to ruin her relaxing dinner party, and then we'd outed her friend as a murderer to boot. I think it's going to take her a while to forgive us for all that.

Brogan lets out a sound very much like a growl, and, despite the seriousness of the situation, it makes my insides quiver just a little bit, as do his next words.

"You even think of laying a hand on Carol ever again and I'll put you down, do you hear me?"

"If you can catch me, Chief."

Another loud crash echoes inside the shop. Dawson lets out a cry of pain, there's the deafening crack of a gunshot, and then a dark shape hurtles out the open door into the night. The wavering light reveals it's Vaughn King, moving faster than his sprightly frame might suggest. By the time Mary and I realize what's happening, he's already halfway across the parking lot. He bypasses his car, which tells me he probably didn't grab the keys on his way out the door. Or maybe he threw them at Dawson.

Brogan and Dawson stumble out the door seconds later.

Dawson is bleeding badly from his right bicep, the thick crimson slide of it winding like a ribbon down his forearm and between his fingers. Mary is at his side at once, pulling off her shawl so she can tie it around the wound.

"Call 911," I advise before taking off after Brogan. I doubt I'll fare any better than the last two chases, but I have to try to help. Brogan should not face King alone. He's proved himself very, very dangerous.

If I weren't getting winded, I'd chuckle to myself. Three chases in the last few weeks. One to catch Bruno, one to catch Tom, and now this.

Bruno lets out a bass *woof*, and then he's off as well, running alongside me for a few moments before he grows tired of my gimpy pace and speeds ahead.

It becomes clear where Vaughn is going after three minutes of dedicated chasing. He rounds the last shop of the strip mall and dashes across the street toward the largest park in Tinsel Pine. It's decorated year-round in Christmas decor, no matter the season, and is one of the largest attractions in town. It boasts the third largest snow globe in the world and sets the record for the number of ceramic reindeer in one place.

I brace my hand on the enormous wooden columns that flank the entrance. They're painted to resemble oversized candy canes. The park beyond looks a little creepy shrouded in gloom, along with the fog that's crept over town in the last hour. I have to keep going. I can hear Bruno's barks and Brogan's shouts further inside.

It's easy to track their progress through the park. Three sets of footprints dot the path. One sharp-edged with a heel, undoubtedly a dress shoe. Vaughn's. The other has a heavier tread and belongs to the boot that Brogan insisted on wearing, even though it doesn't match his suit. I appreciate his foresight now. Bruno's large pawprints bring up the rear.

With a suddenness that startles, the lights flicker on and illuminate the park. "O Come, All Ye Faithful" begins to warble through the night, the multi-colored Christmas lights cast strobing colors onto the snow, and the shadows of a hundred or more reindeer and sleighs loom over everything. The booming *ho, ho, ho* of a nearby animatronic Santa scares the living daylights out of me, and I avoid being clocked in the face by his bell by a margin of inches.

Up ahead, Vaughn is struggling to keep his footing on a patch of slick ground. Brogan is feet away, and stops to plant his feet and raise his weapon.

"Stop right there, King! Put your hands where I can see them."

Bruno gets to him first, ramming his massive bulk into Vaughn's knees. The shopkeeper goes down with a yell and a string of curses, landing on his back in the snow.

Brogan holsters the gun and kneels at Vaughn's side, flipping the man onto his back and twisting one arm into position to cuff him, and then the other. When the cuffs click into place, he gets an arm under Vaughn and heaves him into an upright position.

"You have the right to remain silent," he says, breath coming a little harder after the chase. I'm amazed that he can talk at all. "Anything you say can and will be used against you in a court of law. You have the right to an attorney. If you cannot afford an attorney, one will be appointed for you."

Brogan glances up at me, and then at Bruno. His face finally splits into a reluctant smile. He reaches over and scratches fondly behind one of the mastiff's ears.

"Turns out you were a good boy after all, huh?"

Bruno's tongue lolls out in a happy, doggy grin.

"He's looking for a home, you know," I say innocently.

"And he's quite good in chases. Think there might be a position for him? A one-dog K-9 unit?"

Brogan begins pushing Vaughn back the way we've come.

"I think something could be arranged."

EPILOGUE

The stolen prescription for Tramadol was found in Vaughn King's garbage. It's enough evidence to hold him for suspected murder until a solid case can be built. What no one can deny is his involvement in a diamond-smuggling scheme that's cost his investors thousands, if not more. Even if we can't get him on a murder charge, he's still going away for a long time.

It doesn't take much cajoling to convince Brogan to keep Bruno. After the dog's daring takedown of the perp, Brogan's warmed to the idea of a pet quite a bit. The pet dander still causes his allergies to kick up now and then, but he's decided it's worth the price. Bruno curls contentedly beneath the mantle while Brogan and I settle on the couch. Our date night is on, as promised—just several days late.

I settle the bowl of popcorn between our thighs with a smile and accept a slice of pizza on a drooping paper towel from Brogan. The pooch is eyeing us from his position, possibly formulating a plot to steal a slice of pepperoni before the night is up. We're between episodes, the house is warm, and the sun is just beginning to set outside. It's perfect. Nothing can ruin this night for me.

"Before I forget," Brogan says, standing to cross over to the mantle. There's a wad of paper beneath one of the overturned photos. "I wanted to show you the revised relationship agreement."

A groan slides from my mouth. I know better than to think things like that. I'm just daring the universe to prove me wrong.

"Brogan, I thought that we'd gone over this."

He shoves the piece of paper at me with a grin. "Just read it, Carol. I think you'll like the changes."

I take the papers with a dubious snort before scanning the page. I'm fully expecting to find revised dates and demands from the last contract. Instead, I see only one piece of paper with just a few short sentences typed on it.

Brogan Peterson has instated an open-house policy. The signee is entitled to enter this domicile within reasonable time frames every day after working hours. A dresser has been set up in the guest room for her use if she is so inclined. Peterson solemnly swears to take the signee on a date every holiday, and even agrees to wear a monkey suit on occasion if it is called for.

If these terms are acceptable, could Miss Green please sign the darn contract with more enthusiasm this time?

A laugh bubbles out of me. "You're right. I do like these terms better. But maybe you should make an addendum that states you only take me out on *major* holidays. You'll be taking me out every day if you go with every celebration that the town has."

He quirks a brow, just a fraction. "I fail to see a problem with that."

I bounce up from the couch cushions with a pleased sound, knocking the bowl of popcorn onto its side. Brogan catches me easily, arms winding around my waist at once as I lace my fingers behind his head.

"You are the sweetest man alive," I whisper before I press my lips to his.

I'm not sure how long we stand there, locked in an embrace. He lifts me slightly from the ground with his ardor. The sounds of the episode are muffled background noise, and not even the sound of Bruno munching on the spilled popcorn can ruin the moment.

There's one thing that can, though, and it's the knock that issues from the front door. We pull apart reluctantly after a few seconds.

"Shall I tell them to buzz off?" Brogan murmurs.

"We should probably be polite," I whisper back, though I'm inclined to tell the visitor to shoo and come back when it's more convenient.

"If you insist."

He sets me gently on my feet and makes his way to the door, hand still linked with one of mine. He swings the door open and flicks on the porch light to get a good look at the visitor.

There's a woman on the stoop. From the way she carries herself, I believe she's Brogan's age or just shy of it. Younger than me, certainly. But without the perfect posture and air of confidence to boost my estimation, she looks even younger. Like a mid-to-late thirties soccer mom. She's wearing a tight pencil skirt that hugs a perfectly petite frame. I doubt this woman has ever missed a day in the gym. Her hair shows a little gray at the temples and along the part in her dyed black hair, revealing that she's missed a trip to the salon.

Her eyes are possibly the most beautiful shade of hazel I've ever seen, flirting with the idea of being green near the pupil and edged with a line of dark chestnut around the iris. They flick from Brogan to me, and then down to our joined hands. Her lower lip curls just a fraction as she scrutinizes me. Self-consciousness strikes with a vengeance. I'm not wearing any makeup, my sweats have holes in them, and my shirt is a little too tight, showing all my ample proportions. I'm never as put together as this woman on the best of days.

Brogan's hand tightens on mine to the point of pain. I want to draw my fingers out of his crushing grip, but I'm afraid it'll only make the situation worse. His face has fixed into hard lines, and he stares her down like she's a perp in his interrogation room.

"What do you want?" he demands.

Her mouth slides into an easy, almost flirty grin as she regards him. "Aren't you going to invite me in, Brogan? It's cold out here."

"No," he says shortly. "Tell me what you're here for, then get off my lawn."

"Rude," she sniffs. "I was hoping we could have a nightcap before I was forced to do this."

She reaches into the bag dangling at her side and pulls out a manilla folder. "You've been served. There's a date set at the courthouse on February 14th."

"Fine. Leave."

"Who is this, Brogan? What's going on?"

Brogan squeezes his eyes shut and takes several deep breaths before he can compose his answer. "This is my ex-wife, Sharona."

Sharona? This is the woman who's been dragging Brogan through hell for the last six months? She's so...small. She seems so classy. Not at all what I envisioned. Maybe if I'd actually flipped up the pictures on his mantle and stared into her face, I wouldn't feel so tongue-tied now.

"Wife," she corrects him, flicking a contemptuous sneer at me. "At least, until the paperwork is done. Guess that makes you the other woman, huh?"

"Get out," Brogan growls. "I don't want to see you until the next court date."

Sharona shrugs her delicate shoulders and turns on one high heel to go. She flips her hair when she reaches the end of the sidewalk. She gives him a flirty little wink and blows a kiss in his direction.

"See you on Valentine's Day, lover."

ABOUT WENDY MEADOWS

Wendy Meadows is a USA Today bestselling author whose stories showcase women sleuths. To date, she has published dozens of books, which include her popular Sweetfern Harbor series, Sweet Peach Bakery series, and Alaska Cozy series, to name a few. She lives in the "Granite State" with her husband, two sons, two mini pigs and a lovable Labradoodle.

Join Wendy's newsletter to stay up-to-date with new releases. As a subscriber, you'll also get BLACKVINE MANOR, the complete series, for FREE!

Join Wendy's Newsletter Here
wendymeadows.com/cozy

Made in United States
Orlando, FL
02 September 2022

21883463R00085